Ladygrove

by John Burke

THE DEVIL'S FOOTSTEPS
THE BLACK CHARADE
LADYGROVE

Ladygrove

The Third Adventure
of Dr Caspian and Bronwen

JOHN BURKE

Coward, McCann & Geoghegan, Inc.
New York

First American Edition 1978

Library of Congress Cataloging in Publication Data

Burke, John Frederick, 1922-
   Ladygrove.

   I. Title.
PZ3.B9157Lad 1978   [PR6003.U54]   823'.9'14   78-14539
ISBN 0-698-10933-3

Printed in the United States of America

For
JEAN
who helped conjure strange
things from the forests

What has signs exists, and
what has prophecies will come.

FECHNER
Buchlein vom Leben nach dem Tode

PART I

The Barrier

I

The house stood in a fold of the valley half a mile from the village and divided from it by a meandering river. Beyond the western slope of the vale there rose in sombre cloud shapes the shoulders of the Black Mountains. In that sheltering arm, chequerwork of timber and plaster was sharply etched in black and white against soft blue-green background.

Judith Brobury first set eyes on it one fine spring day in 1887, and could understand at once why it meant so much to the man who was soon to be her husband. Until this moment she had only once seen a trace of nervousness in him: when he proposed to her. Now he was again on edge. Bringing her to meet his parents, he was anxious that they should like her and she like them, but even more that she would like Ladygrove Manor. One day, when it fell on him to become Sir David, and she Lady Brobury, it would inevitably be their home.

Not for a long while yet, she hoped. They had met in London; David worked hard and successfully in London; and they had already chosen the town house they would buy. Herefordshire, the village of Mockblane and the manorial estate were too far away. Later she might be content with the remoteness and serenity of it all. For there was no denying at first glance its serenity and beauty.

'Beautiful,' she said.

David could not doubt the sincere note in her voice. He smiled, and took her hand; and the trap carried them down the hill and across the river to Ladygrove.

On that first visit she was shy and as wishful as he was to please and be pleased. In return David's father, Sir Mortimer, was extravagantly boisterous; while Lady Brobury, fluttery and shrill, made such an effort to put Judith at ease that she agitated everyone, starting impulsive sentences which remained unfinished, and appealing in fits and starts to her husband for confirmation of small points which

9

clearly meant nothing whatsoever to him. They made an oddly matched couple. Sir Mortimer was domineering yet erratic, stumping off at a second's notice and not reappearing until hours later. 'Somewhere on the estate,' his wife would mutter. 'Always up to something.' One might have supposed that she resented his need to keep an eye on his staff and property and would have preferred him attentively at her side; yet when he did sit with her she talked at random, often not looking at him, and rarely listening to him. Once he got up in the middle of one of her remarks and went out of the room, not in a temper but as if his mind had simply ceased to register the sound she was making and hurried off on its own concerns.

But there was no denying their hospitality or their readiness to accept Judith. Sir Mortimer several times put his arm round Judith and squeezed her in a more than paternal manner. 'Deuced good fortune some young chaps have these days. If I were twenty years younger . . .' He chuckled, and Judith wondered – half amused, half ashamed at the thought – where he really went during some of those absences of his, and whether he really needed to lament not being twenty years younger. Lady Brobury, for her part, said 'Thought he was never going to settle down' and asked Judith's preferences for the flower-beds, and talked at length about the rooms which would be set aside here for her and David, not so much signifying approval of their forthcoming marriage as taking it amiably for granted and drawing her future daughter-in-law into the pattern of life at Ladygrove.

Not yet, thought Judith.

'Now, when you next come down, my dear . . .'

When she next came down, Judith was Mrs David Brobury. Not a stranger to be welcomed and set at ease, but one of the family.

She explored, hand in hand with David, the places he had loved best in childhood. 'Margaret and I built a tree house in the wood here.' Margaret was his elder sister, whom Judith had not met: living in Malaya, she was the wife of a government engineer doing something important somewhere in the Straits Settlements. David's scattered references to her burgeoned into the picture of a brisk girl who had been sometimes dictatorial, sometimes derisive, but more often tomboyishly cooperative in his schemes and daydreams. 'I built the house in that elm tree – my first architectural venture, I suppose you could call it – and Margaret furnished it, and we spent hours there making up stories and games. If one of us was in disgrace and went off out of sight, the other never came near the tree house. I knew Margaret would want to be left to herself. And she knew when I was there alone.'

He took Judith's arm and stumbled down with her into a bramble-choked hollow, pulling her close to shield her from scratches, and kissed her.

'And did she stay away when you brought some pretty girl here?'

The grip of his fingers into her arms was as painful as the brambles would have been. 'I always knew there would have to be somebody like you to come and share all this with me. And now I've got you, and I was wrong.'

'Wrong?'

'There's *nobody* like you.'

They went together into the trimly clipped maze half hidden within a grove of oak and ash, between the river and a stream which had carved itself a way down from the hill behind the house. There were some cunning deceits between those yew hedges. Ten or twelve inches higher than the average man or woman, they nevertheless seemed to present no major obstacle – one could surely get one's bearings by peeping through the twigs and interstices? – until one ventured inside. Then there were alleys which doubled back on themselves, and culs-de-sac tantalizingly finishing against the outer hedge or a thick inner clump. Once Judith chose a right turn while David went to the left: it took a great deal of retracing steps and hallooing before they came face to face again and she rushed into his arms.

'Nobody,' he said: 'nobody like you in the whole world.'

Once conquered, the ingenuities of the maze rarely perplexed again. Judith could soon find her way without fail to the crumbling ruin at its centre: the fragmentary wall of a small chapel, with a narrow stone outbuilding set against it, in a fair state of preservation.

'All that's left of an old priory,' David had explained. 'And in the Middle Ages there was a resident anchoress.'

Judith shivered, imagining herself shut away from the world, summer and winter, in a self-imposed incarceration in this lonely valley.

Only once, and that on first reaching it, did she duck her head and venture into the dank interior. There had presumably never been a doorway as such, but through the centuries some stones had collapsed and left an opening with a precarious lintel of two heavier blocks mortared together. The floor was covered with rubble, dried leaves, and lumps of fallen stone.

Judith was glad to escape into the open air; glad to walk with David along the sweeter-smelling rides through the woods and out over expanses of parkland. One afternoon they saw Sir Mortimer in the distance and waved, but he affected not to notice and cantered away beyond the trees. Freed from the necessity of playing the host, he was now going about his own business with as casual an attitude towards his daughter-in-law as towards his wife.

Lady Brobury's narrow face was wrenched by disdain every time he set out; and when he returned she would often stand close to him, like some suspicious teetotaller trying to smell a husband's breath, and then turn away without a word. But they did not quarrel, any more than they showed warmth or shared a joke, an intimate memory or affectionate smile. Nothing Lady Brobury said struck Sir Mortimer as worthy of notice. He interrupted her when he had something of his own to say; and when she chattered more swiftly as if at all costs to seize his attention, he blandly ignored her.

Perhaps indifference was the normal, even preferable state after years of marriage?

Judith refused to believe it. She was too much in love with her husband: more, much more in love than before they were wed.

Yet, ready as she was to share David's pleasure in Ladygrove, there were certain constraints beginning to trouble her in the house, in their bedroom.

Those first nights after their wedding had been a breathtaking revelation. When he had courted her, her body had ached for his but she had not fully understood the ache or its assuagement. At the instant of pain and ecstasy when his flesh first entered hers, she laughed first at the shock of it – laughed so that she would not have to cry – and then with exultation. When it was over she sank into a smug melancholy, sorrowing for women who were afraid, women who could not love, women who would never allow themselves to know this. And later, as the warmth came again and became raging heat again, she laughed again and did not care whether it was seemly or unseemly that she should let her husband know the intensity of her delight.

In Ladygrove, in the still of the rural night, it was different. Her candid passion froze. Because his parents were under the same roof, perhaps awake, perhaps talking about them? It was absurd. Yet for Judith there was, under this roof, something out of true: out of tune. When David's left arm crept round her shoulders and his right hand moved over her, she stiffened. His hand slowed, hesitated.

'What is it, my love?'

'Nothing,' she said. And because she loved him she made herself respond in a pretence which lovingly became almost real – real enough for him to be lovingly deceived.

But she was glad they did not have to live here permanently.

They came again; and again; rode to the village and rode over the hill to another village, on the railway line, and along the river valley and through the Brobury woods and pastures.

They came for Christmas.

It was bitterly cold and there had been snow a fortnight before, but now it had gone and there was a bleak stillness over the countryside. Log fires burned in the hall and dining-room of Ladygrove Manor; the carter brought a fresh consignment of coal from the station; breath puffed in feathery gasps as David and Judith returned from a brisk walk to the invitation of firelight flickering through the tall windows of the terrace.

Two nights after Christmas, warmed with wine and the desire in his gaze across the room, she lured him to bed early and drew him on her, wordless but wanton, so that he and not she was the one who cried out, and she clutched him and abandoned herself to him and what he was planting in her.

For she was suddenly, senselessly, utterly sure that on this night she must have conceived.

He slept. She turned over three or four times, tucking her chin under the sheet and blankets, feeling the cold on the tip of her nose, then burying her head, choking, and pulling herself out again. When at last she was comfortable she was barely asleep, and did not really believe herself to be asleep when the dream began.

She was walking towards the maze as she had done several times before. For some reason there was a darkness of shifting mist all about the grove, but the maze itself shone out as green and clear as ever in that inner glade. She went through the entrace as confidently as ever.

Then she was halted. The way ahead was barred by a hedge which she did not remember. It could not have been there before. Turning to the left, she was confronted by another barrier. To the right stretched a short avenue whose farther end must turn along another path, though she had no recollection of it. She took three steps along the avenue, and found another opening on her left: another cul-de-sac. At its end sat a carved stone statue which she was positive had not been there on previous visits.

She ought to turn back and find her way out of the maze, back to the house and back to bed.

One part of Judith's mind told her she was already in bed. She must force herself to wake up and break the dream. She pushed her arms outwards so that her fingers could brush against the smoothness of the sheet, and so that on one side she could touch David's hunched, warm hip.

Both hands scraped through leaves and twigs in the hedges to either side.

The statue was as high as the hedge: a swollen woman of stone with a tiny head but vast, pendulous breasts, hips thrusting grossly out, and between the legs a voluptuously wide gash. The face was expressionless, with blind slits for eyes and a thin slit of a mouth.

All at once she knew, without daring to look, that other faces were leering out of the yew to left and right, grimacing and urging her forward.

And the stone statue ahead was no longer stone. The lips parted plump and slack. A stunted arm reached out for her, its solid hand opening into greedy claws. The heavy breasts swayed.

'What do you want?' Judith had to shout repudiation into the

14

nightmare. But always in nightmare it is impossible to speak. 'Why me – what do you want from me?' She heard the strangled plea in her own head, but the creature neither heard nor understood. Instead, it slid from its slimy plinth and lurched to meet her. The claw would tear into her, tear life from her, squash it into that dripping maw.

She gagged on a scream; and woke up.

David's arms were around her, he was holding her steady while she tried to thrash her way free. 'What's the matter? What is it, my dear – my dearest? Judith . . . where *are* you?'

She was sobbing helplessly.

'A dream,' he soothed. 'You must have had an awful dream.'

'Yes. No. I mean . . . it was real.'

'This is real.' He stroked her hair and slid his hand between her shoulder blades, stroking rhythmically until her breathing slowed and she let herself sink back on the pillow. 'What sort of dream – what was it about?'

'I don't know.' A fleeting horror dwindled into infinity down a long, long avenue of neatly clipped hedges. 'I don't remember.'

She slept.

In the morning she went resolutely to the maze, refusing David's companionship. Whatever had caused the dream must be banished. Her own pride demanded that she walk to the heart of the maze, slowly, looking defiantly down every alley, and then walk back.

She reached the opening and took one pace in.

It was impossible to take a second.

Judith stole a glance to her right. And one to her left. There were no new gaps, no grimacing faces. And straight ahead lay nothing but the familiar path which, she knew, would fork and then fork again. No puzzles; no terrors. There was no stony monster round that next corner waiting to come to life – waiting for her.

Still she could not advance a step.

The sun shone, the grove was bright and frozen under a steely December sky.

'Let me in.' She said it aloud. 'I must see.'

There was an invisible hand on her chest, holding her back. When she fought against it, as one would fight against a gust of wind, it thrust more forbiddingly and forced her to retreat.

'I'm imagining it. It's all part of the dream.' Did she really say that aloud, or was it indeed part of her strangled, speechless dream?

'But of course,' said David jubilantly when they were back in London and, weeks later, she told him her news. 'No wonder you were restless. All those weird ideas! I thought there might have been some food that disagreed with you. But now we know.'

He waltzed her round the room until it seemed to her that the gas mantles so newly installed went into hissing, flickering protest. Next day he treated her like a fragile piece of china which might shatter if handled too roughly.

'It's so few weeks,' Judith protested. 'I'm in no need of coddling. And as for that nightmare in Ladygrove, I could hardly have been unsettled at such an early stage . . .'

That nightmare. That night. Could the moment of conception be so immediately devastating, throwing her so wildly off balance?

She remembered – suddenly, vividly – that rapacious claw stabbing out to gouge her open and rob her.

When the news of a coming grandchild was broken to David's father and mother there was a swift and unexpected result. Sir Mortimer came post-haste to London. Judith had assumed, a trifle gloomily, that she and David would be summoned to Ladygrove to talk about the future and a choice of names and layette and the best place for the accouchement. Instead, here was Sir Mortimer in their Marylebone home with a glass of brandy in one hand, a cigar in the other, and a troubled look in his red-rimmed eyes.

'You won't bring yourselves to Ladygrove before the child is born.' It was a patrician order. For all his undeniable dignity, his hand shook. Judith wondered how many drinks he had poured into himself before arriving on their doorstep.

David jibbed. 'But father, I'd been counting on a true Ladygrove heir. Born on the premises, as they say.'

'Stay where you are.' Judith had never heard him so fierce and direct before. 'Don't expose him . . . to danger.'

'Dr Treharne up the valley is perfectly capable of –'

'Damn Treharne. More important things to concern yourself with.' Sir Mortimer turned a bleary but authoritative eye upon

Judith. 'You will lie in here – here in London. If you try to come to Ladygrove, I swear I won't allow it.'

Judith felt she should have protested but was overwhelmed by a great, inexplicable relief. Recognizing her thankfulness, Sir Mortimer smirked over another brandy and then another, and a lazily lecherous gleam came into both bleary eyes and he pinched Judith's bottom, and there was such a devilish love of life in his grin that she could only take the pinch as a compliment.

'I was born there,' he confided. 'But they didn't get me. All that offering back, whatever it might be – they didn't manage it. You hear some mad things in this world, isn't it so?' He belched. 'But somehow I was kept away. For all the good it's ever done me.' His face twitched into what might have been puzzlement or a deep discontent. But the gleam was soon back and he was staring brazenly yet flatteringly at Judith's bosom swelling from the olive green satin of her bodice. 'Don't often find myself in town nowadays. Really must treat myself to a stroll. Don't wait up for me – I'm old enough to take care of myself.'

When he set off next morning, bleary and yellow-cheeked, on his homeward journey, he lectured Judith once more. 'Stay here, my gel. Let's have a Brobury born safely in London. Fool the old hag once again, hah?'

Judith asked David what his father had meant. David shrugged it off. It was a Brobury failing to grow wild and irrational in late middle age and talk rubbish. She asked if he, too, would talk rubbish at such an age, and he said he would talk rubbish here and now – sentimental rubbish – and he put his lips to her throat and kissed with mounting eagerness down the breast his father had looked at so appreciatively the previous evening.

She loved him, and felt safe.

Until, six months later, they received the telegram announcing Sir Mortimer's death in a riding accident on his own estate.

Now the estate was theirs.

David and Judith had overnight become Sir David and Lady Brobury. Of course they must attend to the funeral and of course David must meet the family solicitors and discuss the administration of his inheritance.

17

'But we don't have to leave London?' begged Judith.

'It's ours now, all of it. Our home.'

'But this is our home, here.'

'It's not Ladygrove. That's the real Brobury home.'

'Not until after the baby's born.'

'Well . . .'

She insisted. He agreed. They would move into Ladygrove, so much more convenient for the threads he must now unravel and then weave into his own approved pattern. But she should have the baby in London. If that was how she wished it, that was how it should be.

Ladygrove Manor was empty without Sir Mortimer. It needed replenishing, restoring to life. It needed a new generation of Broburys.

Judith apprehensively sought the entrance to the maze, to persuade herself that the dream had died. But the hand thrust her back even more imperiously than before. She took David with her, and he demonstrated how easy it was to walk into the labyrinth and out again – 'There's nothing in there, nothing at all, nothing to be scared of.' But when he took her hand and tried to take her in with him, the pressure forcing her back was so stern and savage that she crumpled to the ground and had to be half carried across the glade and through the trees.

She had been rejected. Hurled out. Yet deep down she was sure that the hand which thrust her back would one day close on her, claim her, draw her in and destroy her.

'Why do I have to be here?' she sobbed at David, who kissed her and sat with her and walked with her and said he understood – which grievously she knew he didn't – and murmured those coaxing little phrases to which he knew she was most susceptible. For the first time ever she wanted to push him away and clutch herself to herself, clutch her swollen body and feel a fretful little kick against her hand.

'What does this place want me for?'

Sir Mortimer had told her that she must not come back, not until her child was born. But Sir Mortimer was no longer master of the house and no longer able to enforce his wishes.

2

Doctor Caspian and his wife came down through Mockblane in the middle of a late August afternoon. The sun was still high as the carriage jolted over the humped stone bridge, but brightness on the western bank was already being sucked away over the river and up the far slope. Evening would settle early on this bank and on Ladygrove Manor.

The horses slowed on the climb to the entrance gates. Bronwen Caspian turned to watch the play of light and wispy shadow on the church tower and on thatched and red-tiled roofs of the village. Glints of sunshine sparkled in the river like fish skimming over and through the ripples.

David Brobury said: 'I'm still not accustomed to being home. Home for good, I mean.'

'You won't find it dull after London?'

'Dull? At school and university I couldn't wait for the vacations. And when I'd set up practice in town, I never lost the opportunity of a weekend, or any weeks I could contrive. Father used to badger his friends to have their houses restored or totally rebuilt so that I could come and work for a while in the neighbourhood.'

They drove between red-brick gateposts towards the timbered house, sprouting red-brick Tudor chimneys too florid and heavy for the roofs above which they soared.

'And now you'll set about refashioning your own house?'

'Certainly not. I've always loved every corner of it, just as it is.'

He was in his early thirties but, thought Bronwen affectionately, at times showed all the lack of reserve of an endearing, exuberant little boy. He was so eager for them to see his domain through his own doting eyes.

'You get a fine perspective of the east wing from here. Remarkable example of over-sailing. Stroke of genius. And that lattice window up there under the eaves – my favourite attic. I used to spend hours moaning and scratching up there, trying to frighten my sister into thinking I was the resident ghost.'

'You have a ghost?'

'Naturally. A very conventional lot, the Broburys.'

'And your sister was duly frightened?'

'Oh, not Margaret. She was always too matter-of-fact to be frightened of anything.'

Caspian looked up in leisurely appreciation as the house loomed over them.

The two men had known each other some six or seven years. When Caspian was at the height of his stage fame as the illusionist and prestidigitator Count Caspar, David had been the architect responsible for alterations to the Cavern of Mystery before the opening of the 1886 season; and after Caspian and Bronwen married, it was David who renovated the house they had taken in Chelsea. Now it was his turn to offer a commission: the Caspians, on their way to visit Bronwen's old home in Wales, must break their journey in Herefordshire so that Bronwen could take architectural photographs of Ladygrove Manor.

The carriage wheels rustled to a halt on the gravel before the house. The sound brought a young woman out on the step.

Judith Brobury held out her arms in welcome. She and her husband were alike in their impulsive gestures, sketching in large parts of their conversation with their hands, sometimes semaphoring so vigorously that one wondered if they might not ultimately strike one another in their animation.

'Bronwen, my dear. Alexander.'

Her stomach, heavy with child, was proudly thrust out as if to balance the bustle beneath her widely draped, swaying, brown and cream cashmere skirt. The baby was surely due within a few weeks at most, but the burden did not appear to depress her: five or six years younger than David, she had a fine sparkle in her cheeks and hazel eyes, and her deep brown hair had lost none of its rosewood lustre.

Her expressive right hand fell and found a resting place on the head of a golden retriever which had come out to stand beside her.

'You ought not to rush out-of-doors like that, Judith.'

The thin but penetrating voice came from darkness within the doorway. David exchanged a little grimace of amusement with his wife, then led his visitors forward.

'I don't think you've ever met my mother.'

'And do keep that dog away from your guests. It has become very treacherous lately.'

The widowed Lady Brobury was standing in the middle of the hall. At first it was difficult, coming in from the afternoon light, to make out her features. Then as Bronwen's eyes adjusted to the change she saw how richly that inner darkness glowed – in chestnut wall panels and in a great oak table polished to glossy blackness. Lady Brobury's face emerged pale and thin-lipped, floating in space, with a strand of grey hair which seemed to slice off her forehead only a few inches above the eyebrows. Slowly she took on substance: clad in mourning, with a black bonnet trimmed with crape, she was an angular wraith reluctant to step out of the obscurity.

They shook hands. Her touch was brief and cold, the fingers snatching away in a few seconds.

'David, do make Judith go back to the chaise-longue. In my day no young woman in that condition would have been allowed out into the cold air.'

'It's hardly cold, mother.'

'Cold enough.'

Lady Brobury led the way towards a door opening out of the hall and was about to lead the way through; then stopped and turned.

'I'm sorry. Of course this is your house now.'

'Mother, really . . .'

But the Dowager Lady Brobury stood rigid at one side while her daughter-in-law preceded her into the drawing-room. David took his mother's arm and at the same time winked and waved Bronwen forward.

It was an airy, welcoming room which came to life as they entered, as if it had been waiting for a long time for a new generation to revitalize it. Tall windows framed a vista of curving valley, lost round a distant out-thrust of green cliff. A line of elms masked the village, save for the gleam of the weather-vane, still catching the sunlight.

'Judith and I have already taken tea. We waited as long as we could, but you were so late. But if you'd care for tea . . . or do you want to go to your room first? . . . David, do look after your guests.'

Lady Brobury was, Bronwen estimated, only in her early sixties; but she affected a painful shuffle, her shoulders slumping under the weight of an intolerable burden – if not of years, then of some indescribable injustice – and when she spoke a plaintive little whine was left echoing on the air.

Parched after the train journey and the drive over dusty miles from the railway station, Bronwen admitted that she would welcome a cup of tea. As David rang, tugging the long bell-pull by the fireplace, his mother turned back towards the door.

'I must be getting back to my little house, then.'

'Mother, you'll stay and have another cup?'

'I can see I'll only be in the way.'

David went with her to the front entrance. Bronwen observed that when she was halfway down the arc of the drive and in full sight of the windows, she had acquired a limp.

'Oh, dear,' said Judith.

Caspian stood looking out, the jut of his trim beard silhouetted against the far hillside. 'We're not putting her out in any way?' And as David returned, he added: 'It must be difficult for her to grasp that your father's no longer here.'

'That's what we tell ourselves when she grows particularly trying. There are times, though . . .'

He checked himself as his wife shook her head at him.

'But I do wish,' Judith admitted, 'that she wouldn't put on such a show of being banished to the dower house.' She smiled ruefully. 'We didn't want to push her out. She could have had her old bedroom here, her dressing-room, her own little drawing-room just as before. But she insisted on moving out.'

'And letting us know how she suffers,' said David.

His hand touched Judith's shoulder. She smiled up at him, and they laughed the absurd irritation of it away.

A maid arrived with a silver tray and silver teapot. Conversation changed to the Caspians' journey and what lay before them in Caernarvon. 'Another case of family homes and old relics,' said Bronwen, and David said, 'Are you calling my mother an old relic?' and they all began to talk at once and it was like the convivial hours they had so often spent together in London.

The bedroom on the south-east corner of the house overlooked a long stretch of undulating parkland ending in thick beech woods. From this height a few village rooftops and a corner of the church were visible. Blobs like grey cottonwool further down the valley might be boulders or browsing sheep. Below the window a busy little stream cut its way down the slope, under the terrace, and disappeared into a plantation beyond which lay the slower river.

Before dinner, Judith suggested a stroll in the garden.

'Take a shawl,' David warned, 'in case mother sees you and comes out predicting doom for the Brobury heir.'

'Come on, Pippin.' The retriever fell in beside Judith and padded beside her across the grass. Bronwen matched her pace to theirs.

Light was fading now from the tip of the eastern ridge. Judith looked up it and suddenly said: 'London's over that way, isn't it?'

'Roughly. A long way over.'

Judith nodded and let out a little sigh.

'Aren't you happy here?' asked Bronwen quietly.

'I . . . oh, I haven't settled yet, that's all.'

'When the baby comes – '

'Yes.' Judith snatched at the idea. 'It'll all feel so much better when the baby comes.'

Behind them David Brobury was explaining something to Caspian, and behind the two men Bronwen was conscious of shrouded hills, rising mountains, and then the lonely expanses of Wales to be crossed before she and her husband reached the coast and Caernarvon. Her homeland, Wales: in which, a married woman now knowing so many new worlds, she was afraid of finding herself a stranger. She wondered if David, in spite of his devotion to Ladygrove, felt altogether at home after having for so long made his home elsewhere. And if he would succeed in making Judith feel at home.

They went deeper into shadow. Oak and ash trees closed in about

23

them. Leaves were uncannily still and there was not the faintest pipe of birdsong. Only the stream chattered a tune over its stony bed. A few yards into the unbreathing gloom, and Bronwen came to one end of a narrow wooden bridge. Outlines at the other end were indistinct but there seemed to be a tidily squared-up hedge between saplings and a tangle of bushes.

'We'd better not go any further this evening.'

Not until Judith spoke did Bronwen realize that she had lagged behind and come to a stop on the edge of the grove.

'Is there some sort of formal garden in there?'

'A maze,' said Judith stiffly.

'Oh, we must explore that tomorrow.'

'If you can.'

'It's overgrown?'

'No. At least, I don't suppose it is. I . . . I can never get into it.'

'You lose your way?'

'I can't even cross the bridge.' Judith sounded tense and unhappy. 'It was all right when we used to visit, but then something happened, and now that we've come to live here . . .' She drew the shawl more tightly about her and turned to meet David and Caspian as they came from the far side of the lawn.

'Mother doesn't have that trouble, anyway.' David's arm pressed the shawl even more closely over her shoulders. 'There's a fragment of old chapel in the heart of the maze,' he explained to Caspian. 'Long ago it was an anchoress's cell, and then sometime in the eighteenth century the maze was built round it – a bit of fashionable landscaping. Mother sits in there by the hour.'

'Doing what?'

'Goodness knows. Perhaps trying to lift the family curse.'

Caspian raised a saturnine eyebrow. 'You have one, then?'

'I told you, the Broburys have all the conventional things.'

'Obviously none of them worry you.'

A slight cloud darkened David's brow. 'Judith is starting to worry a little,' he said with a quickly suppressed hint of asperity. His hand squeezed her shoulder fondly. 'It's ridiculous, of course.'

The dog edged in beside Judith's skirt. From the distance came the clopping of hoofs, the note changing as they struck the gravel within the gateway.

'That must be the vicar.' David released Judith and started up the slope. 'I'd better collect mother from the lodge and bring her in to dinner.'

3

The Vicar was a tall young man with a smooth yet troubled face. It was difficult to conceive that such a girlish complexion ever needed shaving; but where other men might have had shadows of beard on cheeks and chin, he had odd little puckerings under his eyes, dark gashes tugging the corners of his mouth down, and he looked constantly from side to side as if fearing some unprovoked attack. He wore a dark coat which, with its concealed buttons, had more the appearance of a robe, and his hair had been cut in such a way as to suggest a tonsure. Caspian had noticed that after saying grace the Reverend Frederick Goswell had swiftly crossed himself. Such a mannered high churchman, fashionable as he might have been in London or Oxford, was out of place in a rural community like that of Mockblane. One wondered what the villagers made of him.

'And a priest-hole, naturally,' David was saying. 'Some say the ghost is the tormented spirit of a priest who died of starvation before it was safe to release him.'

'And Charles the Second,' said Bronwen, 'doubtless hid in one of your oak trees?'

'We're a bit too far west for that.'

'And the family curse?' Caspian prompted.

Lady Brobury snapped unexpectedly: 'David wasn't born in this house. What could *he* know about it?'

'I believe,' said Mr Goswell, 'we should think rather of family blessings than of curses.'

Lady Brobury melted at once and smiled at him. She still wore black but for the evening had exchanged her bonnet for a lace cap with a long veil pulled back from her gaunt face. It bore some resemblance to a mantilla, and when she looked yearningly across the table she might well have been beseeching an audience with Mr Goswell.

'Such as the blessings,' he went on, 'which our benefactress has bestowed on this parish.'

'I shall continue to do what I can – with my limited means.'

David frowned at his plate.

His mother raised her voice. 'While you are restoring the chancel to its rightful significance, I should like to dedicate a window to Matilda of Mockblane.'

'Lady Brobury! What a wonderful surprise – wonderful gesture!'

Lady Brobury sat up proudly, then winced and put a hand to her back.

David said: 'Mother, it's not healthy for you to spend so much time in that damp old cell.'

'Who says it's damp?'

'You're getting pains in your back.'

'The old trouble,' Lady Brobury sighed.

'Which one, mother?' David asked it in apparent innocence but gave Judith a quick wink.

Lady Brobury rounded on her daughter-in-law. 'You'll find out soon enough. Once you've had children, you'll find out. Never be quite right again.'

'Really, mother!'

'You don't know the pain I suffer. I don't complain, but if you *knew* . . . And now that I'm all on my own – '

'Mother.' David spoke slowly and deliberately. 'You are not all on your own. We're here with you.'

'You wouldn't have come back if I hadn't made you. As bad as your father.' She looked uncertainly, almost apprehensively, up the table as if expecting to find Sir Mortimer still seated in his usual place. The candelabra in the centre shimmered with reflections of its own branched lights, and of the lamp brackets on the walls. 'Your father.' They let her sit in silence for a moment. Then in a burst of fretfulness she went on: 'When I think how he whisked us away from Ladygrove when you were on the way! So inconsiderate. That was what started all my trouble. By the time we came back the damage was done.' She clapped a hand to her side and winced again, more loudly this time. 'But I don't ask for sympathy.'

'No, mother.'

'But if I hadn't gone down on my knees and begged you to come back – '

'You didn't go down on your knees.' David was trying to make an easy-going joke of it. 'You know perfectly well that we came as soon as we heard.'

Lady Brobury sulkily prodded at a slice of roast pork and then, as if recognizing it for the first time, pushed it away. She glared at Judith's plate. 'How you can eat the way you do, in your condition, I don't know. You'll pay for it. I know *I* shall pay for it tonight.' She mumbled her way into self-communing resentment.

Judith took the opportunity of asking Bronwen about old acquaintances in London – about the girl from the Cavern of Mystery who had had twins, about a contemporary newly returned from New York, and about her photography of some friends' children.

Lady Brobury endured this for a few minutes, then emerged from her rumination as testily as she had sunk into it. 'You've come here to take photographs of my house, Mrs Caspian. That is, my son's house.' It was an accusation rather than a question.

'I hope to make a few studies here, yes.'

'An unusual occupation for a married lady.'

'My father was a pioneer in the field. I like to keep up the tradition.'

'Tradition,' Lady Brobury echoed sceptically.

'We're on our way to Caernarvon to arrange for the removal of his collection of plates. My sister wants to sell the house, and we can't let the archives be broken up or inadequately housed.'

'They're so important?'

'My father and I spent many years making photographic records of buildings. Especially those of historic interest, threatened with decay or demolition, so that posterity won't be entirely deprived of all memory of our architectural heritage.'

'So that's what it is?' Lady Brobury pounced on her son. 'You want a record of this house before you start playing about with it. Altering it, altering everything. It won't suit me. I know it won't.'

'I have no intention,' said David, 'of altering anything. Repairs where necessary, yes: alterations, no.'

'Hm. You won't want me under your feet. And I won't want to watch it happen.'

28

Before David could argue there was the faint, remote sound of a doorbell. After a brief pause the butler tapped at the dining-room door and came in.

'Your Ladyship, there's one of the Hoskyn family asking for the parson. Says old Mrs Hoskyn's sinking fast and she'd like him to be there.'

Mr Goswell rose, his pink face lengthening into a sort of lugubrious complacency.

'I was afraid she was not long for this world. I must give her what solace I can. Dear Lady Brobury, you'll excuse me?'

She insisted on escorting him personally to the door. When she returned she was wiping a tear from her eye.

'Such a good man. Such a tower of strength.'

David said warily: 'He still worries me. I don't see our old low church villagers taking to all his Popish practices.'

'How dare you call them Popish?'

'The way he's treating the altar, the form of service, and the way he's encouraging you to set up your own little cult in that damned maze – '

'What do any of you understand? *Any* of you?'

'In this part of the world, folk have always been more used to men like old Haines.'

'Not always,' said Lady Brobury very quietly.

'For enough centuries, anyway.'

'Haines. A man of no insight whatsoever. Your father did right to offer the living to a man of true sanctity.'

'Because you asked him to?'

'When did your father ever pay any attention to anything *I* wanted?' said Lady Brobury inconsequentially. She had not sat down again since returning to the room. Somehow frail and at a loss, she blinked above the candelabra. 'Mrs Caspian. Judith. Let's leave the gentlemen to their port.'

When the ladies had gone, David pushed his chair back and stretched out his legs. 'I'm sorry to have exposed you to such family bickering. Mother does ramble on, and I know I ought to let it all roll over my head – but after these last few weeks of it I'm afraid I'm getting awfully snappish. On Judith's account as much as my own.'

29

He waited until the butler had set the decanter between them and gone out again. 'But you were right: she must find it difficult to accept that my father's no longer here, and we must make allowances and go on making them.' Thoughtfully he twirled the stem of a glass between his fingers. 'She was always a bit vague, and one never knew which way a mood would take her, but the shock of finding my father – '

'She was the one who found him after the accident?'

'I wasn't here at the time, of course. I can only go on what she told me, and by the time I got here she was scarcely able to tell anything coherently. But the coroner – a doctor from up the valley, an old friend of the family – he smoothed things over for her as well as he could, and told me as much as he could. It was simple enough. Father was out riding the bounds of the estate when something must have frightened his horse. It was unlike Jenny to go wild – she's mettlesome, but father always knew how to handle her – but something must have set her off. She seems to have shied off into the woods for some reason, and thrown him. He was dragged by the stirrup through the undergrowth and' – David poured from the decanter and drank deeply – 'rather badly knocked about by some tree stumps and brambles.'

'It must have been terrible for your mother.'

'She remembers so little. Or prefers not to. When he was late coming home, several of the staff were sent out. And mother thought she knew which direction he'd be coming back in, and went there. She can't say how or why, and I don't fancy pressing her.'

'And the horse?'

'She's perfectly all right. A few scratches, but less than I'd have expected. I wanted to have her put down so that mother wouldn't be upset by the memory of it all. But that was one thing she was firm about it: she couldn't bear to blame the animal, and wouldn't let me destroy it.'

If Lady Brobury had managed to be so rational about that aspect of the sad business, thought Caspian, she ought sooner or later to see other aspects in a reasonable light and so shake off her aimless resentments. For the sake of the younger Broburys it was to be hoped so.

'The death,' he ventured: 'no significant parallel with the family curse, or anything like that?'

'Good heavens, no.' David relaxed. 'But of course, I was forgetting. You've always been interested in occult mysteries, haven't you?'

'In the effect of beliefs and obsessions on the human mind, yes.'

'And how they become real?'

'Real to those who so wish it.'

'I don't wish to believe any such gibberish,' said David. 'But you do get these family legends, and a lot of things get passed down and distorted, and I suppose we're all proud of having a little bit of colourful nonsense attached to our name. It becomes like a nursery rhyme which makes little sense in itself but continues to haunt you. Some silly, repetitive little jingle.'

He held his glass up to the light and contemplated the rich radiance of the wine.

'A jingle?' Caspian nudged him.

Self-consciously David recited:

> 'Strife shall be 'twixt man and wife
> Till yielded back there be the life
> Of thy house's first-born son.'

'Meaning the house of Brobury in the family sense,' said Caspian, 'rather than the actual building?'

'That's something we're not sure of. If you allow for the possibility of the original having been in Latin, and then being twisted into English doggerel over the years, it's hard to be sure of any real interpretation.'

'But things have happened – things to illustrate it?'

'Well . . .' David looked momentarily uneasy. 'Yes and no. Some odd coincidences, or . . . oh, I don't know, I can't help thinking some bits of family history have been misread in order to fit the curse from a long way back.'

'How far back?'

David drank, and began a brisk, matter-of-fact narrative as if to cancel out that uncharacteristic flutter of unease.

The tradition of the Brobury curse dated from the dissolution of the

31

monasteries in the sixteenth century, but both family and site were of much older lineage. The first Brobury had come to England with William the Conqueror and, like many a knight granted land and riches in return for supporting the Norman invasion, had built himself a small castle above the bend of the river, incorporating a well-appointed chapel. During a succession of baronial squabbles the castle and its defences had been slighted, and ultimately demolished by royal decree; but the chapel survived as the village church.

To this church came a young anchoress.

In the Middle Ages many a parish acquired its resident holy man or woman. A cell would be built into the outer wall of church or chapel, with a squint through which the recluse could devoutly follow the Mass without being observed by any other member of the congregation. In return for the anchorite's unceasing prayers, food and drink and gifts were laid outside the cell, usually in such quantities that the priest or his bishop would acquire a large share as well as basking in the prestige of having their house of worship enhanced by the presence of such a holy hermit. The church of Mockblane in the Brobury demesne was blessed with the care of a young woman called to her vocation at the age of sixteen, her name coming down through later generations as Matilda of Mockblane. There were no records of miracles, little about Matilda's life or the date of her death, and no suggestion of later beatification.

'But my mother,' said David dourly, 'has chosen to start up a little local cult of her own. Whether she started it before my father died or afterwards – or before Goswell came or after – I don't know. But that Goswell chap certainly connives at it.'

It must have been shortly after the anchoress's death that a new church was built on the other side of the valley, closer to the village. The old chapel and its hallowed cell were offered by the Broburys to a strict sisterhood of Carmelites who maintained a small priory on the slope and declared themselves spiritual guardians of the memory of Matilda. There they remained until driven out by Henry VIII's purge of religious houses. The property was returned to the Broburys, who had diplomatically opted to edge away from the old faith and support Henry in his dispute with Rome. The nuns were cursorily evicted, and reputedly the Brobury of the time behaved with especial callousness to the Mother Superior of the Order. It was she who, driven mockingly out into the turmoil of a world from which she had so long been secluded, was said to have laid the curse upon the family.

' "Offered back",' mused Caspian. 'Offered back in what sense, and to whom?'

'That's another of the puzzles. Earlier members of the family thought that if they could solve that, they'd be able to avert the consequences of the malediction. In recent times we've paid little attention.'

'And hoped it would pay no attention to you, either?'

David laughed wryly. 'If one refuses to see a curse working in everyday incidents or misfortunes, does it in fact work?'

'You'll have to quote a few examples before I'd risk an opinion on that.'

'Well, looked at in a certain light . . . if one's in a gullible frame of mind . . . there have been some events uncomfortably close to the prophecy. I mean, if you're determined to *see* such a closeness . . .'

The first Brobury son to be born in the Tudor house built on the conventual foundations married young and soon found his marriage turning sour. After bearing him a son, his wife had the child secretly christened as a Catholic and then, when power came into the hands of Bloody Mary, contrived to have her husband handed over as a heretic and burnt at the stake. Was this the offering demanded by the curse? Or could the dedication of the son to the Church of Rome be taken as that offering back? But that same son managed in Queen Elizabeth's time to fall foul of *his* wife, who with her lover engineered his being sent to the block for treason. For a while the lands were confiscated by the Crown; and during that time the surviving children and their children, living elsewhere, were untroubled.

Later the property was restored to the penitent, Protestant Broburys. The next two cases of firstborn children delivered on the premises were of daughters, unaffected by the malediction. One of the girls, of devout turn of mind, also secretly returned to the Catholic faith and vowed herself to the life of a recluse, half hoping that such voluntary dedication might lift the cloud from the family. But the next time a son was born into the household the pattern had a grim

33

familiarity: happy marriage turning to disaster, crazed wife ruining her husband and bringing about his early death.

At last the family quit Ladygrove Manor and left it in the hands of a bailiff, building for themselves a Queen Anne mansion on the farthest extremity of their estate. Here they suffered no more tragedies. Until, early in this present century, the house was gutted by fire and, newly married and unable to afford rebuilding, Sir Mortimer's father moved back into the old home. He had not been born at Ladygrove himself – 'And so,' observed David Brobury, 'seems to have been immune. But my father was born here.'

Caspian framed a dozen questions, each stumbling more provocatively over the last. He could not tell whether David's coolly dismissive telling of the history was genuine or whether it hid some unadmitted apprehension. He chose his words with care. ' "Strife 'twixt man and wife",' he quoted. 'Was there a lot of disagreement between your father and mother?'

'Not that I remember. The usual domestic squabbles, I suppose – and mother did tend to harp on the fact that she was rushed away just before I was born – but on the whole I think they got on amicably enough. There were no great upheavals: certainly not when I was around.'

'And your own child is going to be born here?'

David hesitated. 'There's no good reason why not, but . . .'

'You see no reason why not,' Caspian probed.

'*I* wasn't born here, so my wife won't turn on me.'

'So you do to some extent believe in the family curse.'

'I only meant that if there were such a thing, and it sticks to its pattern, I have nothing to fear.'

'And what about your son, in later life? If the child should be a son, that is.'

David's eyes were evasive. 'Now you sound like Judith.'

'Judith doesn't like the idea?'

'You know how women get at this stage. Or so I'm told. This is our first time. But they do indulge in all kinds of fancies, don't they?'

'Some fancies deserve to be humoured.'

'In fact, I've more or less promised to take her away and look after her in London. I still have a lot of business to settle in town, and I

34

could be there with her. Though I'd still prefer an heir born under this roof.'

'If she will feel more confident in London – '

'But why shouldn't she feel confident here? It's our home.'

'Yours,' said Caspian gently. 'Not yet hers. You must be patient.'

David gave a rueful nod. 'Yes, yes. I'm afraid you're right. The trouble is, I've had to deal with so many things at once. Taking over the estate and learning the ropes, and at the same time winding up the practice in London – and then there's my mother, and Judith in the state she is.'

'Which is the most important?'

'Judith.'

'Quite so.'

'It's good to talk to you, Alex.'

'I only state the obvious.'

'When one gets tired and confused, the obvious often gets lost.'

They sat for a moment in companionable silence. Then Caspian said: 'You haven't been putting ideas into Judith's head? I mean, worrying her with too many jokes about the family curse?'

'She'd never take such stuff seriously.'

'She may be more susceptible than you think. People can be coaxed, or can coax themselves once given the initial tug, into believing many a strange fancy to be real.'

'These old wives' tales couldn't be real.'

'You're not absolutely convinced of that, are you? Generations of your family have believed, or half believed. Such a half-willing body of people can, shall we say, half-will a thing into existence. A state of mind can create an illness – can virtually create a physical entity.'

'You're saying we've dreamed up our own curse?'

'I'm saying that if successive generations have a fatalistic conviction that events will happen in rough parallel to events which have happened before, or are supposed to have happened before, then they may well be forced into happening. We may explain it by saying that even by the law of averages there must be a number of families in this country who suffer runs of bad luck and get more than their fair share of disaster. But there may be something more positive behind it all. What I'm warning you of is the danger of drifting into acceptance of such a sequence.'

'I won't, I promise you.'

'And help Judith. Let her know that – '

'I love her,' said David simply. 'And that she knows.' He pushed his empty glass away from him. 'On which note, I think for her sake and Bronwen's we'd better join the ladies and rescue them from mother.'

'I thought you were never going to give up drinking and gossiping,' Lady Brobury greeted them. 'I hope David hasn't been boring you with too many of his business problems, Dr Caspian? If only he could get out of the habit of running to and from London, he might not *have* so many problems, eh?'

She sat slumped in an armchair covered in flowered chintz, with a cushion stuffed into her back so that she was hunched forward. Beside her right elbow was a cabinet behind whose glass doors were arrayed a couple of dozen pottery and porcelain pigs, snouts all pointing towards her chair. Judith was wriggling uncomfortably into another position on the chaise longue. Bronwen raised her eyes to her husband's: wide green eyes, glowing a welcome below the glow of her coiled auburn hair.

'My back,' said Lady Brobury. 'Sitting up so late. My back. And what about Judith? David, you have no consideration. I'm sure we'd all have liked to go to bed early. Though I did hope there might have been time for Dr Caspian to perform for us.'

Caspian stared. 'I'm afraid I – '

'After what your wife has been telling us, I thought you might entertain us with a few card tricks.'

'I'm no longer as skilled in that sort of thing as I was.' He managed a mock reproachful glare at Bronwen. 'It's ages since I practised.'

'Or some mind-reading,' said Lady Brobury petulantly. 'I'm given to understand that is a very popular diversion in the best salons nowadays.'

'There, too, I'm out of practice.'

'Then what *do* you do, doctor?'

Again he exchanged glances with his wife. Tired after the journey, she stifled a yawn and then wrinkled her nose at him in apology. Their minds brushed drowsily together. What did he do, indeed; what did the two of them do? If they had demonstrated their true talent for mind-reading, Lady Brobury would undoubtedly have been horrified. From the time of their first encounter in the distant Fens, through marriage and work in London, they had shared and developed the ability to commune in silent, secret conversation – and to probe into the consciousness of others. It was a rare gift; and one to be treated delicately. They used it as sparingly as possible: the psychic drain was physically exhausting, and even the most loving relationship could not have survived the naked reality of undisguised mental revelations. There had to be secrets, mysteries, reservations between a man and woman; and others should be free from tele-pathic trespass save in the direst emergency.

But as bodies grow sleepier, so minds relax their grip and float, drifting towards one another, bumping and grazing, sometimes caressing and sometimes jolting away from a sudden unexpected contact.

Caspian felt Bronwen very close to him. Lazily she accepted the touch of his hand on her arm, although there was a wide stretch of carpet between them. Her skin lovingly warmed his fingertips. Her mouth puckered into a secret little smile.

Lost in the abstract pleasure of it, Caspian had failed to answer Lady Brobury's question. Now she pushed herself up from her chair.

'If you'll be so good as to fetch me a lantern, David, I'll see myself home.'

'Mother, you know I always walk to the lodge with you.'

'There's no need for you to put yourself out. Not for me. Good-ness knows, I ought to know the way well enough by now.'

Caspian and Bronwen felt the rise and fall of other minds; felt Judith, too, wanting to yawn and saw her turn her head away to conceal it; felt David's wry irritation at his mother, and, out of the blur of Lady Brobury's own random thoughts, her sharp stab of pleasure at knowing she had irritated him.

For no apparent reason Lady Brobury said: 'Children. Such messy little things – and precious little help when they grow older. You'll see, my dear.' Vaguely she nodded at Judith. 'Oh, you'll find out soon enough. When I think what I went through with Margaret and David, and now . . .' She clutched at herself. 'My back's never been so bad as it is tonight. Never. I shan't get a wink of sleep.'

'Mother.' David stood beside her. She pretended not to notice. 'I'll wager that when he arrives you'll be the first and worst at spoiling your grandson.'

'Or granddaughter,' said Judith mildly.

Before another word could be spoken, Bronwen and Caspian were shaken by a screech of words through their minds, as harsh and startling as a railway engine letting off steam on a quiet country siding.

No, it has to be a boy. Has to be, this time. Born in this house.

As if momentarily aware of their reaction, Lady Brobury blinked from one to the other. Then she muttered something about her wrap and how she must say goodnight and how unnecessary it was for David to accompany her.

At the door she paused. Fumbling through memory for some remark which must have been made by somebody else and was only now becoming clear, she said:

'But of course it will be a boy. You'll see.'

⚜ 4 ⚜

The sun rose above the eastern ridge and brought to life first the roof and then the dormer windows of Ladygrove Manor. Poising itself on the crest of the hill, it seemed ready to roll down the slope and set the village ablaze. Shadows fled across the fields. Under the trees of a distant knoll the ground brightened with a dappled pattern of leaf, branch and sky. Leaning from her window, Bronwen looked out upon an idyllic English pastoral scene: timeless, unchanging, steeped forever in a tradition as radiant as the sunshine. The village chimneys puffed out trailers of smoke. Nothing else moved. It was all as still as one of her own photographs: captured, immutable, safe forever.

Bronwen was out and about early, making the most of the morning light to take pictures of various elevations of the house. This, too, belonged and could have belonged nowhere else: infused with the spirit of generation after generation of Broburys, each timber a sturdy limb of the family itself.

She included a study of the dower house, a lodge of more recent date than the main building, with a steeply pitched roof like a tall hat thrust down on a squat head and body, its thatched brim creased over almost to the shoulders. At one juncture Lady Brobury appeared under the diminutive porch, watching Bronwen focus her hand camera, and then dodged back indoors like some superstitious native afraid of losing her soul if she were trapped in a photograph.

For more ambitious work Bronwen still preferred the definition she could achieve with the old collodion process, but the need to take along a mobile dark-room, tripod camera and other unwieldy material made travel difficult. To lighten the load on this journey she had brought a hand camera and automatic changing boxes of dry plates which could be developed when they reached Caernarvon instead of having to be treated on the spot.

Lady Brobury chose not to join them for lunch, so conversation was freer. Bronwen noticed that whenever old friends in London were mentioned, Judith's expression grew wistful. But then David would hurry on boisterously with some story about a neighbouring landowner, and remind her of a farmer's children who had taken an especial fancy to her, and Judith was smiling again.

'She hasn't even ridden over the whole estate yet,' he said to Bronwen. And Judith said, 'And won't be doing so for a while yet,' and David went on enthusiastically, 'But there's so much to see, there are such splendid tracks up and over the hill, you haven't even begun to discover your own possessions.'

They sat and talked too long. The light had gone from the house and grounds disconcertingly early in the afternoon. When she went out again, Bronwen found it was too late to attempt pictures of the maze or the anchoress's cell. She considered going in for a preliminary survey, but then decided to save it all for the next morning. It would be impossible today even to guess how the light would fall and what her best viewpoint would be. Instead, she announced her intention of taking some pictures in the village. There might be some interesting cottages, and she wanted a closer look at the church.

David supplied a pony and trap, and Caspian came along to drive and help her with the heavy plate boxes.

On the far side of the river, over the humped bridge, they were back in brightness. Roofs gleamed, and light struck along little alleys against plastered walls and out in slanting fingers across the dusty street. A cloud of midges danced above a cottage garden. Somewhere a dog barked incessantly. Seen at close quarters the village was less compact, less of a picturesque whole than when viewed from a distance. Houses were set at odd angles, with little apparent concern for the lie of the land or the street. Some frontages were crumbling: laths and twigs showed through. A woman on her knees was scrubbing the doorstep of the inn, the Brobury Arms. A suspicious face appeared between lace curtains, watching the two strangers; but further up the street a man in a stained smock touched the brim of his billycock hat and said 'Art'noon' in a deep, affable voice.

They stopped by the churchyard wall. Caspian tethered the pony to a post by the lych-gate and gave Bronwen a hand with her equipment.

The church had a sandy red tower with a pierced parapet: sturdy, unpretentious and, as a shaft of sunlight fell on it, as ruddy and wholesome as a cider apple. Within, the nave was higher than one would have estimated from outside, with octagonal piers and a simple but powerful hammerbeam roof.

Caspian had hardly set the plate boxes down by the inner door of the south porch when footsteps hurried up the path and followed them into the cool interior.

Mr Goswell said: 'How delightful to meet you again. Now you can see for yourselves the work we're struggling to accomplish here.'

He led them proudly up the aisle towards the east end. Beyond the tower, with two plaited bell ropes looped up to either side, polished candlesticks gleamed on the altar within the chancel. Mr Goswell bobbed a brief genuflection and looked raptly up at the plain glass of the east window, ornamented with only one red and green heraldic medallion in the centre.

'That is where Lady Brobury will see her new window. Without her generosity I do not know how God's work could be done.'

He waved at the north side of the chancel, newly plastered. The south wall was still in process of being cleaned. Lumps of plaster had fallen to the floor, and in one corner was a heap of fine white dust. The restoration had revealed a faded fragment of wall painting, and to one side was a memorial plaque into whose letters the mortar and plaster had been so compacted as to leave barely distinguishable outlines.

'For years,' intoned the vicar mournfully, 'this was used as a store-room. Can you credit it? A store-room and cloakroom. The cleaners kept their brooms and buckets here, the congregation hung their coats here; and the parson conducted the entire service with his back to the altar.' He shook his head, inviting their incredulity. 'But now, with Lady Brobury's beneficence . . .' He spread his arms to encompass in a slowly sweeping gesture the restored ceiling, the cross and candlesticks, and the unfinished work on the south wall. 'But I must leave you to make your own observations. And your – ah – photographic studies. If in due course you have any prints to spare, I'd be most grateful if copies could be contributed to our parish records.'

Bronwen assured Mr Goswell that he should certainly receive copies, and he went off with a loping stride, glancing back once as she set about her preparations.

Light through aisle and nave windows was good enough for some pictures of the interior as a whole, and the pulpit and organ. Then Bronwen moved into the chancel. She would try, none too optimistically, to photograph the hazy mural and that indecipherable plaque inside it.

'I'll leave you to it for a while,' said Caspian. 'Perhaps I can find you some other interesting subjects.'

An old woman was snipping grass away from the borders of a grave. Its grey headstone was dwarfed by a veritable temple of red brick near-by, built hard against the south wall of the chancel within high iron railings. Two small openings to either side of a studded oak door were barred by ornamental iron grilles, and above the door itself a stone arch bore simply one name:

BROBURY

Caspian strolled past it and contemplated the vicarage, a square Georgian house reached by a gate between its garden and the churchyard.

The woman tending the grave turned to squint at him. 'You a friend of parson's?'

'We've met. A very brief acquaintanceship.'

'Hm.' She bent over her task again, but as he continued to stand there, turning his attention to the names and inscriptions on the nearer gravestones, she found more words. 'If you were any friend of his, you'd tell him it's high time he found himself a wife.' The shears she held shrieked discordantly against the stone. 'Where's the sense in having a house that big, and him not married?'

'It must be quite lonely there, yes,' Caspian agreed politely.

'Old Mr Haines and his missus, they had a whole clutch of little 'uns. Knew what life was like, they did. Not natural, living there alone.'

She lowered her head, stole him another curious glance, and then worked her way round behind the headstone.

Caspian left the churchyard and walked to the end of the village street. From here a well-trodden path led to the river bank. Here the river narrowed and there was another, smaller bridge with a hard-packed earth surface carrying the path to the far side. A beech planta-tion hid Ladygrove Manor and marked the rim of the Brobury estate for a quarter of a mile, giving way then to a long arc of wooden fencing. Caspian looked back. If Bronwen finished her work and came out of the church, she would be able to see him between the widely-spaced cruck cottages at the end of the village. He crossed the bridge and stood in the shade of the trees.

Water plopped gently against the bank. In the village the dog went on barking, but less insistently. From within the wood came a deeper note, a murmuring which became a snuffling, and a rustling and crackling over leaves and twigs.

Caspian stared along the sun-speckled track between the trees.

Dark shapes hunched their way around a bend in the path. There were three, four, and then a dozen. They snorted and grunted their way towards the open. Heads dipped and greedily thrust into the beech mast; but a shout from behind drove them grumbling on their way again.

The leader raised his snout. Tiny eyes glared at Caspian. For a moment there was a threat of the whole herd of swine charging for-ward. But when they did come on it was still reluctantly, as before, grubbing for a last mouthful of food as they moved. They were like no pigs he had ever seen in this country. With coarse brown skins like small wild boar, some of them had spiky little tusks, and their square snouts were those of central Europe rather than England and the Welsh Marches.

Now they were all about him, jostling and grunting. Bringing up the rear came a stocky, broad-shouldered man who stopped within the shadow of the wood the moment he saw Caspian.

When he forced himself to come out, glowering at the ground, he proved to be a weatherbeaten countryman of thirty or more sum-mers. He wore corduroy breeches and a greasy corduroy jacket, and his cap was pulled down above dark, bushy brows. He sidled his way past Caspian with three jostling hogs between them.

'Good afternoon,' said Caspian.

43

The answering grunt might as well have come from one of the animals.

'An interesting strain,' Caspian attempted. 'Whose are they?'

The man's pace slowed. He debated whether to answer, then said: 'The lady's.'

'Lady Brobury's? I didn't know the estate went in for pig breeding.'

The man glanced slyly back as he plodded on his way. His face was not as coarse as his manner: for all the lowering shagginess of his eyebrows there was a keenness and arrogance in his features which went ill with his clothes and shambling gait. 'Ceridwen,' he said. Or something sounding like that.

A Welsh name, surely. There were plenty of them in this part of Herefordshire, and perhaps the Dowager Lady Brobury was of Welsh stock. But it was hardly proper that her swineherd would be so impertinent as to refer to her by her Christian name.

Returning to the village to collect Bronwen and listen to her account of the afternoon's work, he gave the incident no further thought until that evening. Sitting in the drawing-room before dinner, his attention was caught again by the collection of china pigs.

'The estate supports a very unusual strain of hogs,' he commented.

Lady Brobury brightened at once. 'Oh, you've seen my little herd?'

'Very unusual,' said Caspian again.

David said: 'Another of mother's little occupations. I think she started it just to keep Evan Morris out of mischief.'

'Nonsense. What mischief could poor young Evan possibly get up to?'

'He's a sullen sort of customer. Something peculiar there. I wouldn't care to cross him, I must say.'

'My pigs,' Lady Brobury said grandly to Caspian, 'are unique. Bred from a very old strain, almost extinct in Britain. I'm determined to preserve it and build it up again. And David's not going to stop me.'

'Mother, when did I ever stop you doing anything?'

Without deigning to reply, Lady Brobury turned to Bronwen. 'And how has your picture-making progressed, Mrs Caspian?'

'I hope the results will be satisfactory. Tomorrow morning ought to be enough for the remaining subjects, if the weather holds. Then we must be on our way.'

'But you don't have to leave immediately.' Judith's tone was imploring. 'Surely you can stay on a few more days?'

'We'd love you to stay, you know that,' said David.

'Please.'

'Mrs Caspian has already told us,' said Lady Brobury, 'of the important tasks waiting for her in . . . now, where was it?'

'Caernarvon,' said Bronwen.

'Good gracious, so it was. Caernarvon.' Lady Brobury enunciated the syllables with mounting disbelief.

In the morning Bronwen announced her intention of going into the maze. David glanced quickly at his wife, and said as casually as possible:

'You'd better show her the way in, my dear.'

'David, you know I can't – '

'Perhaps when you have to act as guide you'll find your imagination – '

'It's not imagination! There's . . . something there. Something or somebody.'

He bent over her and kissed her and held her for a long moment. 'Just see,' he begged. 'Just see if it makes any difference when Bronwen's with you.'

David went off with his bailiff to spend some hours on the home farm. Bronwen took her camera and, with Judith at her side, set off across the lawn, round the rose-beds, and down the long slope to the grove. Caspian brought up the rear, carrying another box of plates.

Behind them, birds fussed in the eaves of the house, and there was an occasional chattering flurry of martins. From the grove ahead came no sound but that of the stream.

Bronwen went in under the trees and once more reached the end of the bridge. From the corner of her eye she saw that Judith was faltering. Bronwen put one hand on the flimsy rail of the bridge, which she could now see consisted of little more than two planks above the swiftly running water. Judith stayed a few feet back.

The outer hedge of the maze was clear and neat in a shaft of sun-light. Its full dimensions were masked by clustering ash trees and the broad body of one ancient oak, but between branches Bronwen could make out a jagged stone tooth jutting up from the centre.

'That's the cell?' she asked over her shoulder.

Judith edged closer. Caspian's tall, reassuring frame was dark against the distant black and white flicker of the house.

Bronwen stood to one side. 'Are you going to show me the way?'

Judith mutely, pleadingly, shook her head.

'It looks straightforward enough,' said Bronwen. 'From here to the outside of the maze, anyway.'

'It . . . gets more difficult. Even to get near.'

Bronwen and Caspian stood quite still. Judith stared unhappily across the bridge into that corner of bright glade.

She took a step forward.

Bronwen and Caspian let their minds relax into a soothing swell of nothingness, so that they should neither urge nor alarm Judith. It took, incongruously, a great effort not to concentrate: simply to wait, and not watch, not prod, not reach out a helping hand or even the suspicion of a helping thought.

Judith reached the end of the bridge and tried to put her left foot on it.

Now Bronwen felt the strain. She did not turn to look at her husband, but in every mental and physical fibre she sensed that he too was thrumming with it. They let their minds waken slowly and concentrate slowly, warily on Judith.

The pressure built up. They were one with Judith, feeling as she did the firm thrust of two hands against her shoulders; against their shoulders. With her they struggled to walk forward – so easy, to take a few paces across that bridge and walk on into the glade and enjoy the teasing puzzles of the maze – and with her they fell back a step. And another. The hands which held them back, forced them back, were not rough or aggressive; but very sure and very power-ful.

Judith whimpered, let herself sag against a tree, and it was over.

'You see? I can't do it. I can't get near it.'

She did not know how close they had been to her, how deeply

46

embedded in her they had been, but somehow she was sure they would understand and sympathize.

'What makes you think you can go no farther?' Caspian asked carefully.

'There's some force that won't let me. You don't know what it feels like.' They did, but would not betray the fact. 'It's always the same now. There are other places I don't like, and would sooner not go into – like the priest-hole in the house – but I can make myself do it. Not here.' She looked round. The stream tinkled pleasantly enough, the leaves were bright and dark green and the world shimmered and yet was deliciously still. But Judith shuddered and said: 'There's something waiting. Always out of sight. Under that tree, perhaps, or deeper into the wood. Ready to step out if I persist in trying to reach the maze.'

'Has anything, or anyone, ever stepped out? Anything you could actually see?'

'No. But if it didn't, it would still somehow be there. Waiting for me to stumble over it.'

'Just after we arrived,' Bronwen recalled, 'you said something about it not having always been like this.'

'When David first brought me to Ladygrove I could go in and out of the maze whenever I felt like it.'

'And found . . . ?'

'Nothing out of the ordinary. A fragment of old chapel wall, and the ruin of a cell built against it. Full of leaves and débris. And the maze was easy enough to penetrate, once you'd worked it out. But then it all went strange.'

'When did that begin to happen?'

Judith closed her eyes briefly, not so much in an effort to remember as to shut out something which only she could see, and did not wish to see. 'Soon after I knew I was going to have a baby.'

'How soon after?'

She opened her eyes again. Horror, or the memory of it, stirred in their depths. 'The very day after I . . . after it happened. Or I thought – I was *sure* – it had happened. I had a . . . a dream about the maze, and next day I went down there – down here – and couldn't get in. And then, later' – she blushed a demure pink – 'I felt unwell in the

47

mornings, and got a dizzy feeling, and it grew even more impossible. David thinks it's all part of my condition, of course. Like the
walnuts.'

'Walnuts?'

'Didn't I tell you' – Judith was cheering up, laughing at herself –
'I've had a terrible craving for walnuts these last two months?'

Bronwen smiled a response but went on looking along the line
of the bridge, pointing towards that mysterious yet innocuous-
looking stretch of hedge only fifty or sixty yards away.

She said: 'Well, I've no hunger for walnuts and I don't feel in the
least dizzy. I imagine I'm immune. So I'll go and take a few pictures.'
She beckoned Caspian closer, and tugged the strap of the plate box
on to her shoulder.

Judith was tense again. She watched as Bronwen set foot on the bridge.

No hand thrust Bronwen back. There was nothing to bar her way,
nothing for her to stumble over. She felt the planks creak beneath
her feet; and walked on.

Halfway across, the plate box swung heavily against the rail. There
was a sharp crack. And beneath her feet there was a louder creaking,
and then something like a muffled pistol shot. Her right foot slid
forward and downward. She felt the world giving way under her.
She flailed out wildly with her left hand, but still was toppling forward. A splinter of rail tore her wrist. Suddenly her knees were in
the water and when she let the camera crash down on to the stones
her knees, too, were jarred down on to those hard, unyielding lumps.
Above her Caspian was shouting. She glimpsed a broken plank
swaying above her left shoulder. Then he had splashed into the water
beside her and had an arm under her armpits, heaving her upright.

'The camera – the plates!'

Roughly he bundled her up on to the shallow bank, and turned
back to retrieve the camera and the box.

Judith was motionless, staring fatalistically down.

Bronwen blundered to her feet, squeezed some of the wetness
from her skirt, and winced as her hand brushed across her knees.

'At all events it can hardly be called a malevolent spirit if it saved
you from that,' she said ruefully to Judith. 'Especially in your condition. A pity it didn't take a similar interest in *me*!'

Caspian turned the camera over to reveal a wide crack down one side. When he shook it gently there was a faint clatter from the lens.

'And that's the only one I have with me,' Bronwen lamented.

A faint breeze sighed down the slope, chill through the dampness of her clothes. The three of them headed for the house, Judith staring fixedly at it as if afraid to take her eyes off their goal.

Lady Brobury stood waiting by the corner of the terrace.

'Whatever has been going on?'

Caspian told her.

Her tongue clicked along the back of her teeth. 'The footbridge? Really, how inconsiderate of you. It's not meant to carry that sort of weight.' But her eyes were sparkling with rheumy glee rather than anger as she studied the damaged camera and the plate box. No concern was expressed about Bronwen's sodden, uncomfortable clothes. 'So you didn't get in after all.'

With stiff politeness Bronwen said: 'We had been intending to call in briefly on our return journey and deliver finished prints. Perhaps at the same time I'll be able to polish off the remaining subjects I can't take today. I shall bring some of my father's old equipment with me. And who knows?' She smiled encouragement at the dejected Judith. 'By then I may be able to do a portrait of the next Brobury.'

'I may not be here. David has promised to take me back to London in good time.'

'Nonsense,' said Lady Brobury. 'Of course you'll be here.'

Caspian stood beside Bronwen, his hand on her arm, urging her to hurry towards the house and a change of clothing.

She held her ground for a moment. 'I'd still like at least to see inside the maze before we leave. There must be some other way of reaching it.'

'Forty or fifty yards outside the gates,' said Judith dully, 'you can take a path to the right and get to the grove that way.'

'But I'd prefer you not to,' said Lady Brobury.

Caspian's tug was more insistent.

'It is one of the few places,' Lady Brobury went on, 'where I can still be sure of some privacy. I should prefer to keep it that way.'

49

'I'm sorry. I had no intention of – '

'Just one little place I can call my own.'

Bronwen let Caspian steer her away. As they plodded up the slope they heard Judith saying wryly: 'It's private enough, goodness knows. I couldn't even cross the bridge today, let alone reach the entrance.'

Lady Brobury's airy reply was almost lost on the breeze. 'When you're ready, you'll find it easy enough.'

5

The day after David had driven the Caspians to the station he announced his intention of setting out early to learn all he could about the leases of his various tenants and the state of their accommodation. He would have to work hard for a couple of days to make up for time lost in entertaining their guests.

'Time lost?' Judith was incensed. 'It was a joy to have them here. They made me feel almost civilized again.'

She had not meant it to sound hurtful, yet once it had been snapped out she was glad of the sound of it.

David said placatingly: 'I was glad to see them. We wouldn't have invited them otherwise. But the work of the estate has to go on.'

'Work. All work and no play?'

'Judith, my love, when has it ever been like that for me – for us?'

She remembered accompanying him on many of his architectural commissions, provoking him with comments and asides which he would often dismiss and then summon back, gratefully conceding that she had hit on some important point. At home in the evenings they would share views, and she was glad to have contributed something. She felt so close to him in everything. Now he was throwing himself into his new responsibilities with the same characteristic single-minded enthusiasm; and if she was to share this new preoccupation, she needed to see things at first hand.

'Couldn't I come with you this morning?'

'My love, it won't be just this morning. I intend to be out all day.'

'I've been with you all day before now.'

'It's not quite the same, now.'

'You don't want to be bothered with me.'

'Judith! You know how much I'd like to have you there to turn to. And that's how it will be, later. But it wouldn't be wise as things are, in the – '

'In the condition I'm in!' She mimicked her mother-in-law's inflections.

David looked startled, then put his hand over hers. Her fist clenched, curled up in his grasp. He tried to squeeze it.

'My dearest, you know full well you couldn't face a whole energetic day out with me.'

'So I must face a whole day alone.' To her horror Judith heard another echo of Lady Brobury – the whine of self-pity and reproach in her voice.

'Which will be good for you. You've been talking a lot and looking after Alex and Bronwen, and staying up late. I'd have thought a lazy day without a care in the world would be just the right cordial for you.'

'One day you're blaming me,' she nagged, 'for not having seen even half the estate, and next you're – '

'When have I ever blamed you?'

'Only a few days ago, when Alex and Bronwen were here.'

'I wasn't blaming you. I was holding it out as something still in store. You'll be asked to do your share as soon as you're fit, never fear.'

He was so patient and reasonable that Judith wanted outrageously to hit out at him. The force of her discontent alarmed her. What malicious imp was goading her from the back of her mind? All she knew was that if he said condescendingly, just once more, anything about her state and about understanding why she was so unsettled, making allowances which she didn't want made, she would scream something dreadful at him. And enjoy it.

With an effort, staving off the danger of his saying any such thing, she opened her hand to his. 'Oh, pay no heed to me. You're right, of course you are.'

He kissed her, and she almost flew off at his patronizing manner: a kiss, and the sort of pat he might have bestowed on a pet animal, and the obvious relief in his eyes as he prepared to set out.

No, he didn't want the burden of her company.

Disconsolate, she wandered out across the garden, veering sharply under the shade of the trees to avoid an encounter with Lady Brobury, who had come out of the lodge to contemplate the sky. Cloud hung on the ridge with a threat of rain; but no rain came, and the cloud did not move.

Automatically Judith made her way to the end of the shattered bridge. She was alone, very much alone.

No, that would never do. She mustn't, wouldn't let herself fall into lamentations like Lady Brobury's.

If Bronwen could only have stayed a few days longer she might have been able to help. There was a mysterious strength in her, a tie between herself and Caspian stronger than the closest intimacy between any ordinary man and wife. Judith felt that if both of them could have walked beside her, adding their forces to hers, they might have overcome her irrational inability to walk into the maze.

Noticing that Lady Brobury had retreated indoors, she skirted the wood and reached the end of the drive. Pippin, who had been aimlessly sniffing below the terrace steps, pricked up his ears, twitched his tail, and came hopefully bounding after her.

The path into the woods, down the road from the gates, was somewhat overgrown, but the dog nosed its way in and Judith was able to brush her way between nettles in his wake.

At least, for a hundred yards or so she made good progress. Then, some distance from the glade and the maze, the pressure of a slowly rising wind caught her full face. It began to push her back. She lowered her head so that she could fight a way forward. Until, as she had known she would be, she was forced to a standstill.

The dog was looking back, wagging his tail, waiting for her to catch up.

'No,' she said. 'No, it's no use.'

The moment she turned away on to a narrower track leading at a tangent from the glade into the woods above the river, the resistance eased. Pippin, crashing through fern and ragged bushes, took a short cut which brought him out on the path ahead of her once more.

David had been right. She could not have faced a full, active day. Already she was breathless, and the child within seemed to have swollen and put on weight extravagantly in the past twenty minutes. Judith leaned against a tree. Pippin sauntered and lolloped around in a wavering circle, exploring the undergrowth.

Then his head jerked up. His muzzle pointed, his legs were braced.

53

His faint, querulous whimper was ready at any second to become a growl.

Somewhere there was a rustle and a snapping of twigs.

Pippin growled.

Now Judith heard the heavier thudding of feet and a snuffling in the secrecy of the wood, coming closer and gaining in bestial power.

Pippin barked.

The face which nosed round a bend in the path was squashed, vacuous and menacing. Like a monster gobbling its way out of a hedge. Judith tried not to cry out. Then there were more faces, shifting within one palpitating mass which might at any second divide into a score of demons ready to rise on two legs and come screaming at her.

A howl formed and grated in her throat. A chorus of squeals drowned it out. Hard square snouts and savage tusks shaped themselves out of shadow into the uncertain light.

Pippin's barks grew frenzied, and he hurled himself into the middle of the oncoming mob.

Grunting and squeaking rose almost to a whistle. Pippin yelped. Surrounded, he snapped at an enraged hog and then was heaved aside. Judith forced herself forward, stumbling to his rescue, shouting and waving her arms.

She was within a few feet of the herd when the hand was against her chest again. She tried to beat away an invisible arm and wrist, but was thrust inexorably off the path and against a tree.

There was another shout. The swineherd, driving a few stragglers round the corner, hurried into the battle. His stick rose and fell against the haunches of a huge sow. There was another chorus of squeals as he stormed his way through. One brawny arm plunged, he caught Pippin by the collar, and then was belabouring the dog with his stick.

'Stop it!' Judith tried more desperately to break the spell; but was still held off.

There was a final thwack of the stick. Then the swineherd literally tossed the dog clear by the scruff of its neck.

'Get that thing out of here.'

'How dare you? Beating the creature just because it – '

'Because it was let loose on *her* animals, that's why.'

'You have no right – '

'Haven't been told I've got no right, not by Lady Brobury.'

'*I* am Lady Brobury.'

The sunken eyes gleamed with insolent malice. 'Ah. Well, I suppose y'are as well, ma'am. Your ladyship. But you'd still best keep that dog out of mischief, else her other ladyship won't be best pleased.'

Pippin cowered at Judith's feet. The swine surged past, with one tusker looking as if he might stray and risk another charge. Judith tensed. By her ankle she felt the dog trembling. But the herd went by as if guided along an invisible wall, thumping past only a few inches away.

Evan Morris, resuming his place at the rear and urging them on, slowed as he drew level with her.

'No need to be afraid of 'em, your ladyship. They ain't ready yet.'

'Not ready – for what?'

He quickened the pace, flicked his stick along some wobbling rumps, and drove the herd off down the shaded woodland path.

She wanted to pursue him, wanted to demand an explanation. But Pippin was whimpering, and when she put her hand on his collar he strained towards the way they had come, towards the gates and the house and safety.

Within the gates, Judith turned to approach the lodge. The wicket gate was shut, but at the end of the short paved path the front door under its little porch was open. A pair of secateurs and a trug half filled with cuttings lay on the path near the patch of herb garden. Judith reached for the latch and went in.

Other cuttings and a number of twigs were laid out on the wide window-sill to the left of the door. Judith glanced at them; and was conscious of something trying gently to turn her away, not so much pushing this time as tapping her shoulder in an attempt to distract her.

'No – please, no more.' She said it aloud, and the sound brought Lady Brobury to the door.

'Judith, have you started talking to yourself? A very bad sign. Do come in and have some sherry wine and a biscuit, and talk to *me*.'

'No, really, I – '

'We've got to look after you. Now come along in.'

Judith took a step forward. Was it her own reluctance to share half an hour with her mother-in-law which prompted the warning voice in her head, telling her to turn back?

'You're not having another of your silly turns, are you?' said Lady Brobury. 'Oh, do come in and stop fussing, there's a good girl.'

Pippin, edging in through the gate, was attracted by the glimmer of a dragonfly across his vision. He sprang like a puppy, made a wild snap in mid-air, and finished up against the wall, narrowly missing the window and flailing out with one leg. Twigs on the sill were sent flying in all directions.

'That insufferable dog! I shall insist on David doing something about it. Since Mortimer's death it has been . . . oh, it's quite unmanageable.'

Judith found that without hindrance she had followed Lady Brobury into the cottage. Something had silenced the warning voice. Pippin slouched in behind her and curled up before the hearth, keeping one mournful eye on the older woman in readiness for a hurried departure if it should prove advisable.

Looking at his wary head, Judith considered mentioning the incident with the swineherd and his charges. But Lady Brobury was fussing over the draught from one window and trying to persuade her to move across the room. 'Now you know what I have to put up with. Something will have to be done about it, I keep asking David, and still I'm left sitting here in that draught. It's no wonder my neck gives me so much trouble.' Judith was too tired to make a fuss. She would speak first to David, and see what he made of it.

Sitting here in the lodge made her, if anything, more stiff and uncomfortable. All at once she longed for the solitary comfort of her own drawing-room. After the glass of sherry and two sweet biscuits, she made her excuses and went back to the house. She would do all the right things, all the things her husband and his mother were repeatedly telling her to do: putting her feet up on the chaise longue, pushing a bolster into the small of her back, making sure the doors were closed against draughts and the long curtains drawn just far enough across the windows to shield her from that direction, too. Then she would try to read. There was a new volume of stories by Henry James which she had been promising herself she would settle to, now she had so much enforced time on her hands. But she found it hard to concentrate. For the tenth time she reached for some creased, out-of-date copies of the *Illustrated London News* and leafed idly through them.

A flicker of movement above the page caught her attention. Facing the window, she glimpsed the swineherd heading for the lodge with a menacing, purposeful step.

Judith had lunch sent in on a tray. She decided to have a nap immediately afterwards; but was somehow not in any way surprised when Lady Brobury arrived, quivering with indignation.

'That dog! What's all this I hear about that dog savaging my animals?'

'It was very much the opposite. Those dreadful creatures tried to tear Pippin apart.'

'Because he attacked them.'

'He was . . . trying to protect me.'

'Protect you? Heavens above, protect you from what?'

'We didn't expect a herd of pigs to come rampaging round a corner like that. I was frightened.'

'Of pigs? Whatever next?'

'And your swineherd,' blazed Judith, 'was no help. He was insolent, he made no attempt to intervene, I could have been . . . could have been gored to death, for all he cared.'

'Nonsense.'

Judith knew she had exaggerated slightly, but she was in no mood to be told off like a naughty child. 'You'd take that insolent oaf's word rather than mine?'

The lines in the corners of Lady Brobury's mouth tightened. Then she gulped, and with an odd meekness which was almost an apology said: 'I trust him. I have to.'

'Mother, you mustn't let him have too free a hand.'

But now it was Lady Brobury who wanted to be done with the conversation. Hurriedly she changed the subject. 'When do you expect David back? Perhaps you could both come and have a glass of wine with me before your dinner, both of you.' Which meant that Judith had to say how much more sensible it would be if the three of them dined together – an invitation demurringly, then off-handedly, accepted.

When David did come home, Judith said without preamble: 'I must get away from here. I can't endure much more.'

'My dear, there are weeks to go yet.'

'I want to be in London, where I'll feel safe.'

'Safe? We know the baby can't be due before – '

'It might come early. I don't want to be stuck here at the mercy of the local horse doctor.'

'You're being a bit unreasonable, my love.'

'Your own father forbade me to bear the child at Ladygrove.'

'Father had some strange notions. We agreed – '

'We agreed,' said Judith, 'that you would take me to London in good time and occupy yourself with rounding off business interests there. You promised.'

'But it's too soon. I have a lot of things to tidy up here before I can spare the time to go to London.'

'Then I shall go on my own, and you can join me when it suits you.'

'Judith – what has happened to upset you?'

'Your mother is coming to dinner,' she said frostily. 'Among the things which need tidying is yourself.'

The moment the door closed behind him she felt a twinge of panic. If this bickering became a habit – and in her present state of mind that would be all too easy – he might protract those rides of his across the estate, disappearing on unknown errands as his father had done and seeking other pleasures.

All the more reason why she should flee to London to recover and be refreshed.

At dinner Lady Brobury was unexpectedly quiet for the first fifteen minutes. Then, equally unexpectedly, she came out with: 'Judith, I've been worrying about these unpleasant sensations you've been troubled with.'

'Let's not encourage talk on that subject.' David risked a smile at Judith to show he meant it jokingly.

58

'I've been most inconsiderate, brushing it aside.' His mother twisted a corner of her napkin into the beginnings of a knot and then let it unravel. 'One tends to forget one's own troubles as one grows older, you know. I've never been one to dwell on my own aches and pains.'

'No, mother.'

'But before I had you,' said Lady Brobury, 'I suffered much the same discomfort. I felt I was being pushed out, pushed about – *kept* out.'

'Out of where?'

'Wherever I wanted to go. Judith's quite right. There's something in this house, something that's belonged to the place for too long. We must face it. If only,' she said plaintively, 'I had been given the chance of facing it then, instead of being dragged away, just as David wants to drag *you* away, my dear – '

'No,' said Judith. 'I'm the one who wants to go. Just to go and have the baby, and then come back.'

'It'll never be settled that way. Never be ended.'

David silently consulted Judith, who found herself unable to respond. He bent towards his mother. 'How can it be settled, then?'

'We'll exorcize it, whatever it is.'

David sat back, appalled.

At last he said: 'I've never heard anything like it.'

Judith's mind was in confusion. The mere idea of exorcism was so strange – so much a part of a forgotten and discarded past – that she could not see any present-day meaning in it. Yet she wanted to know. If such things had worked once, long ago, might they not still work? If there was something tangible and evil still haunting Ladygrove Manor, such an ancient curse might most readily be cured by an ancient antidote.

'It can do no harm to try,' said Lady Brobury.

'It could do a great deal of harm.'

Judith said: 'If there's something here that can be dismissed, it would be a relief to have it dismissed. And if there's nothing, then no harm will be done.'

'Get rid of it,' said Lady Brobury. 'Mr Goswell will know what to do. The house can be cleansed once and for all.'

'You two sound as if you were calling in a sweep to clear the chimney of soot.'

Judith was disturbed by her eagerness to be allied with Lady Brobury. Allies, against David? But eagerly she said: 'All right, let's think of it like that. Just like that.'

David did not smile. 'If there's a ghost here, and if it has been here as long as the stories make out, why was it not exorcized before? Because there's no such ghost – or because the ritual didn't work?'

'Conditions could have been unsuitable,' said Lady Brobury. 'Or the procedure could have been mismanaged. All I know is that we are going to do something about it. In the morning,' she said peremptorily, 'you can drive me into the village and we'll consult Mr Goswell.'

'No,' said David.

The two women stared.

'I will not take you to consult Goswell,' he said. 'And as master of this house I forbid you to meddle with exorcism or any other such foolishness.'

'David, you sound so pompous.'

'I'm sorry, but I'll have no part in this. And nor will you. Is that understood?'

The rest of the meal passed in silence, until Lady Brobury coughed over her glass of hock and said it was unfair to set her on edge like this, speaking in that way so that it went straight to her stomach and now she wouldn't sleep a wink all night.

Judith slept very few winks. Estranged from David, not touching him, she stared up into the darkness. A few words uttered in different corners of the house and perhaps along the rim of the maze: what could be wrong in them? If they proved strong, strong enough to wipe out the incubus which this house had, as Lady Brobury said, suffered too long . . .

In the morning the post brought a letter for David.

'From Margaret! She's in Hereford, arranging a school for the children. We must invite her over.'

'That will be nice,' said Judith coolly.

Lady Brobury, when acquainted with the news, said: 'Oh, she'll come in her own good time. She was never one to put herself out for others. She did not even trouble to attend her own father's funeral.'

'Mother, by the time she had received the news, and set out from Penang – '

'Her only interest now will be in what's coming to her through the will.'

'I want to see her about that,' said David. 'Let's get all the loose ends tidied up.'

If he talks about tidying anything else up, thought Judith, I shall burst into tears.

'So,' he went on, 'I'll drive into Hereford, take her to old Fosdyke's office, and go through the papers with her. I'll stay the night, and see if I can bring her back here for a few days. It'll depend on whether she's got the children settled, of course.' He turned to Judith with a loving plea in his face. 'She'll be company for you. Take your mind off things.'

Judith did not trouble to argue.

Next morning she stood in the doorway watching him until the trap had bounced over the bridge. The moment it had turned and disappeared into the village street, Lady Brobury was hurrying from the lodge up the drive.

'We'll do it while he's out of the way,' she said with conspiratorial glee.

'Do what?'

'Fetch Mr Goswell, of course. This afternoon or this evening, whichever he decides is most propitious.'

'You mean we're to go behind David's back?'

'It'll all be over in no time. As straightforward as sweeping a chimney: he said so himself.'

'No, I couldn't . . .'

'Do you want that pest out of this house or don't you? You're going to have to live here the rest of your life, remember.'

'Why didn't you try to drive it out when you were living here?'

Lady Brobury looked vaguely about, then tilted her head in the direction of the distant church. 'Can you imagine that old fool Haines . . .? No, of course you never met him. But conditions weren't right in any case, and now they're right. I'm sure every-thing's ready.'

'Ready? What makes you – '

'We are going to do our best,' said Lady Brobury. 'Will you accompany me in the carriage, or must I visit Mr Goswell on my own?'

Doubtful and filled with a sense of disloyalty, Judith went with her.

The Reverend Frederick Goswell was speechless for a full minute after Lady Brobury had completed her airy request. Then he said: 'You seriously mean you wish me to . . .' He stopped, dodging away from a concept so disturbing. When he tried again, he faltered again: 'I have studied the rite, naturally, but I hardly thought . . . doubt very much whether . . .' Finally he found a solution to absolve him: 'I am quite forbidden to carry it out without permission from my bishop.'

'That low churchman?' snorted Lady Brobury. 'He'd be most unlikely to grant it.'

'Then I must not proceed.'

Lady Brobury drew herself up superbly. 'Surely you do not need reminding, Mr Goswell, that your benefice is administered by the Broburys? Your church is a Peculiar, coming under our jurisdiction and not that of the bishop.'

'That is true, but . . .' Goswell sighed, floundered, and clutched his lapels as if about to deliver a sermon. But already there was a speculative gleam in his eye. He was longing to experiment – to dabble, thought Judith. Again she felt a twinge of conscience, and wished David would return to make a decision and make them all abide by it.

'This evening, then?' Lady Brobury was saying.

'I shall require time to meditate, and prepare myself.'

'This evening, then.'

Judith found that she was shielding herself from guilt by deliberately picking on those aspects of Mr Goswell's appearance and behaviour which could be construed as dramatic rather than devout. His gestures grew lavish and more histrionic. Having thought himself into the part he must play, he was bent on playing it to the full. She remembered an evening with the Caspians a year ago, when Alexander had on the spur of the moment slid into his rôle of Count Caspar, his movements becoming instinctively more expansive while he smoothly perplexed his audience and made them laugh and gasp at his sleight of hand. Goswell tonight was playing the magician, too. She tried to make a joke of it to herself when he insisted on having the lamps dimmed and swung a lantern, like a slowly swinging censer, in the centre of the hall. But to him it was no performance. He was in deadly earnest.

So was Lady Brobury. She stood well away from the vicar but watched his every move. When he went through a door murmuring to himself she followed, maintaining a regular distance between them. Her face was rapt. She mouthed secret little words as her own contribution to the ritual.

After a preliminary tour of inspection and appraisal, the Reverend Frederick Goswell returned to set himself solemnly in the centre of the hall. He raised his eyes and spoke in a clear, ringing voice. He was addressing not the two women but some vision floating in far space.

'We are here to cast out the diseased spirit of this house. Not to wrest demons from any person herein, but only to rid this place of its unhappiness.' He lowered his gaze commandingly. 'Let us pray.'

After the Lord's Prayer had died away into the silence, he opened his breviary and lifted the lantern so that he could read out the first lines he set eyes on.

The silence was chill and unreal. The servants had been told to stay below stairs unless sent for, during what Lady Brobury had referred to as 'a private discussion', and might, in that stillness, be thought all to have fled away into the night.

Mr Goswell placed himself experimentally before the panel which opened into the priest's hole.

'I exorcize thee, most unclean spirit, incursion of the enemy, every spectre, every legion . . .'

After a few minutes he began to mount the stairs, intoning his incantations over and over again until the syllables became a sombre music without meaning or change of stress.

63

'Hear, therefore, and fear . . . procurer of death, destroyer of life . . .'

At one stage he stopped on the landing, looking down, and in his own voice said beseechingly: 'Will you not rest? Seek eternal rest.'

Judith could have sworn that she heard the breath of a sigh. Lady Brobury, motionless, appeared to have heard nothing. She in her mourning and the vicar in his long dark habit were like two pious black crows, faintly mirrored in the panelling against the sway of the lantern's light.

Something as flimsy as a cobweb brushed against Judith's shoulder but then was gone, unable to get a purchase.

Goswell opened the door and the three of them paced out into the cold of the garden. Faint starshine silvered the treetops. As they approached the grove, Goswell was making strange, convoluted motions with the hand holding the breviary. He stopped at the end of the still unrepaired footbridge; and his words now lost all meaning. It took Judith a moment or two to realize that he was no longer speaking English. To what would have been the dismay of his usual congregation, he was intoning the exorcism in Latin.

'. . . *proditor gentium, incitator invidiae, origoa varitiae, causa discordiae, excitator dolorum. . .*' He sang on, insistently and emphatically repeating '*causa discordiae, causa discordiae*'.

Lady Brobury's half-veiled face swam against the flicker of leaves. From her trance she was straining to add a power of her own to that of the vicar. In the eerie light she seemed incongruously to be directing him, setting the pace for every word and gesture.

'*Adiuro te,*' he exhorted the unanswering shadows, '*cum metu et exercitu furoris tui festinus discedas* . . .'

Thrice they walked up and down the bank, parallel with the shrouded grove, then made a long circuit of the garden and returned to the house. Judith wondered what the villagers would make of it if any of them chanced to glimpse the little procession, or one of the servants disobeyed orders and peered out – or what story some skulking poacher might take home to Mockblane.

Back indoors, Goswell knelt and prayed. Then he stood up, straining to his full height, and unleashed one final storm of words.

Judith heard a sound which was no sound save in her own head.

Not true – before God, not true. She was sure someone had held out a hand to her, but when she turned there was nobody there. Nobody, nothing. Nothing save for a strange distortion of light and shade in the panelling behind Goswell. As he raised the lantern yet higher, the shapes twisted in on one another. For the briefest of instants Judith could believe that she saw the dissolving outline of a woman's face, a despairing, imploring face pinched in by a coif which tightened until the features deliquesced into the restful glow of the woodwork. Arms seemed to be skeletally spread wide in a last appeal. But they could only have been the reflections of Mr Goswell's arms, stretched wide as his voice rose and then fell.

He was drained, exhausted by a more than physical exhaustion. Lady Brobury turned the lamps up and led the way into the drawing-room. It was silent and bleakly empty, as if someone had gone out and drawn the air away through the open door: someone who would not be coming back.

Lady Brobury tugged the bell-pull. Mr Goswell had come there fasting, and after the ordeal admitted that he would welcome a slice of game pie and a glass of claret.

'I think,' he ventured, 'we have succeeded. It has departed.'

Lady Brobury's head was on one side, listening.

'Yes,' she said. 'There, now.' She beamed at Judith. 'Now you'll be all right. You'll see.'

Next morning Judith made her way apprehensively down the drive and out of the gates. At the beginning of the path she hesitated. There was no sound, no whisper of movement along the edge of the grove.

And no bird sang.

She set out along the path. Nothing touched her or warned her back as she drew closer to the glade.

At the entrance to the maze she stopped and took a deep breath. Then she stepped one step forward. And another. Without the slightest hindrance she walked to the fanged ruin at the centre of the maze.

PART II

The Prey

Around the next corner she would meet him. She was sure of it. They had become aware of each other in a chime of telepathy like a single resonating bell, so high-pitched that it had to insinuate itself into the brain on a level above and beyond hearing. Even in the years before he came into her life she, the seventh daughter of a seventh daughter, had experienced moments of such precognition when she had known a few seconds before a friend appeared just who that friend would be, preparing a greeting before they met face to face. But it was infinitely more delightful when the encounter was a lovers' meeting.

Bronwen quicked her pace.

Lurching in towards the kerb, a farmer cracked his whip above his horse. The gig slid out again and across the road. It would reach the corner at a speed and at an angle which displayed the driver's conceit rather than his skill.

At the same moment Bronwen, silently greeting her husband as he neared the corner where they would meet, glimpsed through a multitude of conflicting impressions a dray which had crossed his vision. Returning empty from a delivery, it was rattling erratically over the cobbles in the middle of the road and jolting the driver from side to side.

Bronwen and Caspian were, in sudden fearful unison, in two places at once. They saw simultaneously the collision there must be. Saw the angle at which gig and dray would converge; saw that the farmer must be thrown off and down, under the iron-hooped wheel of the dray.

Saw that the farmer would die.

'No!'

Caspian blurred in Bronwen's consciousness. He was leaping sideways, clutching, hauling himself up and grabbing the drayman's arm. She felt his hand as if it were her own, getting a grip on the reins. Hoofs skidded on the cobbles; the dray slithered sideways.

The drayman was shouting.

Round the corner came the gig. The farmer swore as he missed the end of the dray, aslant against the pavement, by inches. But he did not reduce his pace: cursing, he thrashed his horse on out of sight.

Bronwen's concentration on Caspian's tussle around the corner had driven her into collisions of her own: one with an elderly lady who leaned on her umbrella to regain her balance, and one with a lolloping youth who cannoned into her and scraped his knuckles against the nearest wall. She hastened round the corner to rescue her husband from a torrent of wild Welsh malediction. Her own contribution rose keening in a Cymric *hwyl* into the face of the awestruck drayman, who knew his match when he met it.

'He'll never understand,' she said as they made their escape, 'how lucky he is not to be seriously injured. Or to have a horse with a broken leg.'

'Nor will the other one know that by now he ought to be dead.'

She took his arm and they walked with due circumspection back to the house.

There was not a great deal left to be done. Most of the remaining furniture had been put into a local sale, save for items which Bronwen's sisters wished to keep or offer to some of the Powys cousins. Several of these paraded through the house on the pretext that they 'Just wanted to see, like, if there's any little thing I'd like for a souvenir', but really to inspect Dr Alexander Caspian. He was foreign in their eyes, fuelling a broth of respect and amusement which at times incensed Bronwen and at others warmed her to thankfulness. 'Fancy you marryin' our Bron, then!' She was so glad that he had indeed fancied marrying her. A marriage of true minds – and of bodies with a taste for truth. Dismantling the dark-room in which she and her father had worked so assiduously, labelling the scores and scores of boxes preserving his finest plates, she felt a wistfulness for days when the two of them had been here together;

70

but it was an undemanding, unregretful nostalgia, incapable of competing with the sheer reality of her husband's presence.

The last photographic task carried out in this house had been the developing and printing of the Ladygrove subjects. On the whole they were satisfactory, though her attempt to capture the mural and inscription turned out as obscure as she had expected.

Caspian riffled through the prints. 'I wonder if we ought to post these to David instead of presenting ourselves there on the way back.'

'But they're expecting us.'

'I had the impression that Lady Brobury the elder would be well content never to see us again.'

'Whereas Lady Brobury the younger,' retorted Bronwen, 'pleaded with me to come back.'

Caspian plucked meditatively at his beard. 'You're worried about her, aren't you?'

'Aren't *you*? Don't deny it. You felt those weird emanations just as strongly as I did.'

'We went there so that you might take photographs,' he reminded her; 'not to offer advice on psychic matters. Unless invited, it is not our policy to intervene. That is still our policy, isn't it?'

'We weren't invited to intervene in that near accident half an hour ago. We saved one man from death and another from probable injury – without being asked.'

'That was an emergency. An alarm signal. Involuntary reaction.'

'David and Judith are our friends. Aren't we allowed to act voluntarily, against a long-drawn-out danger?'

'What danger?'

'I feel – '

'I feel,' he said, 'that you should abandon your packing pro-gramme and come out with me this afternoon. You've been spend-ing too much time stirring up the dust and gossiping with your relatives.'

'You make it sound as if they were both the same thing.'

'Aren't they?'

In the early afternoon they crossed the straits to the isle of Anglesey and looked back on the grey palisade of Caernarvon's castle wall, its battlemented towers stern and steady against the sky, their reflection unsteady and shivering in the water. Rain clouds threatened from the west, rolling in from the ocean and darkening the island. But they broke on neither coast nor town: thickening and sinking, they blanketed the tops of the mainland mountains.

Caspian and Bronwen took a winding road making a leisurely, unpredictable way towards the heart of the island. After they had been walking for twenty minutes a dolmen on a hummock, some distance off the road, offered an obvious vantage point. They climbed a stile and followed a path which reached the foot of the hummock and then reverently circled it. As Caspian gave Bronwen his hand and helped her up the slope, wind moaned faintly through the gaps below the capstone. They stood by the ancient megalith and looked down on a small dell and undulating pasture beyond.

Jagged slivers of stone stuck out from the sides of the dell, blunted by earth and grass. Wind whipped the top of the dell, but down there the blades of grass were still. Bronwen poised herself and ran down. The slope was steeper than she had thought, and reaching the bottom she almost sprawled over a protruding stone slab which might once have been the footing for some Celtic hut, or the end of a burial chamber set beneath the dolmen.

Caspian shuffled down more cautiously.

The place was desolate; but they were out of the wind, private, secluded.

He began, at first playfully and then with mounting desire, to fondle her. He was on one side of the hollow, she the other, but awareness of his body and his caressing hands and tongue grew stronger against her and within her. She let herself sink to the ground while he stood erect, smiling his love into her eyes. When he thrust into her they were as closely entwined as if they had been at home, naked, on a warm bed.

I love you.

They played every variation of love that their telepathic powers could devise; touching and seeking, achieving a peak of ecstasy without physical consummation.

Father me a child.

He swelled within her and she sought to draw him in deeper. But of course there would be no child. Not yet, though she knew intuitively in every pulse of her being that this was the day of the month when she was most likely to conceive. On such days it was wiser to play the game of remote, mental, teasing love.

For the first time Bronwen felt a spasm of resentment against the man around whose passion she was so passionately wrapped. Judith Brobury was close to her time, ready to bring forth a child. A man and a woman, loving like this, ought to see the physical fruits of such a union . . .

There will come a time.

Caspian's promise, torn from the turmoil of his mind, was true . . . yet not enough.

Bronwen, impaled by a final frenzy close to anger, twisted a few feet along the ground, and came to rest against the stone slab.

At once they both went cold. Her breath was drawn out of her. And Caspian withdrew from her body in swift pain, leaving her empty and with cold searching into her.

When he could speak he said: 'What is this place?'

She put a hand on the stone to support herself. He moved closer, kicking against a lump in the grass. It jerked free: a sheep's skull, bleached to the whiteness of smooth stone, one eye socket staring upwards, momentarily a caricature of a squashed and improbably elongated human head.

'The Celts used to cut off their enemies' heads,' said Bronwen abstractedly, 'and bury them beneath altars or stick them on posts and on the entrances to their forts.' She thought of the long ages that had made the Celts, from prehistoric hunters with their stone axes and arrowheads to the men of bronze and iron, subjugated when their gods and goddesses were banished by the Roman despoilers, yet somehow never defeated, in spirit somehow never annihilated. 'And they put heads into sacred wells and temples to promote fertility.'

The word and its undertones brought Judith Brobury to mind. Still attuned to his wife's thoughts, Caspian caught the tenor of her longings and shied away from it. Silently they went back up the side of the dell to the bleak dolmen.

'This must have been one of the last Druid bastions before the

73

Romans put Anglesey to the sword.' She surveyed the landscape. 'The stain of the massacre hasn't faded.'

'Not one escaped?'

'Roman chroniclers boast that the cult was exterminated. It was one of the few indigenous religions they refused to assimilate or tolerate. If any got away, it must have been into the Welsh mountains, or some valley unknown to the Romans where their secrets could be preserved.'

'They had few secrets by then. Caesar,' Caspian recalled, 'knew a lot about their practices. "If a wrongdoer escapes them"' – he half closed his eyes, searching through memory and conjuring the text off the page – ' "they will even slaughter the innocent. If a human life is not given for a human life, the ruling gods cannot be appeased".'

They made their way back to the road.

'Patterns.' Bronwen, too, spoke aloud, for now they were veiling their innermost thoughts from each other. Discussion now was ordinary, matter-of-fact.

'You see some design – something perpetuated?' he asked.

'Giving back a human life because of . . .' She faltered, confused. 'Haven't we heard something about *giving back* very recently?'

'If you're trying to force a connection between arcane Druid lore and the vague traditions of Ladygrove,' Caspian said, 'you'll have to invent some pretty strange theories.'

'I only meant that in all religious settings, on all ancient sites, there are repetitions of certain elements – '

'At Ladygrove,' he said severely, 'the elements should surely be agreeable rather than disruptive. The devout anchoress, the priory of contemplative nuns – what could be more peaceful and reassuring?'

'Judith hasn't been reassured.' They had almost reached the water's edge before Bronwen ventured: 'Do you suppose a family curse, however intrinsically crude and muddled, could be carried on like . . . well, like some hereditary taint in the blood? So that the minds and bodies of successive generations are gradually warped without their realizing the danger?'

'People who wish to talk themselves into believing nonsense,' said Caspian dismissively, 'will undoubtedly finish by believing nonsense.'

74

But she sensed that he was restless, as he rarely was: restless because of a suspicion at the back of his mind that something was wrong – something too indeterminate to be coolly analysed, summarized and filed away.

Not our policy to intervene . . .

When they got back to the house, where crates and boxes were piled in the hall and the large, bare front room, he went to the set of prints they had left on the mantelpiece. She knew, somehow, that he was going to pick out the dim grey picture she had attempted in the chancel of Mockblane church.

He brought it closer to the light from the window and set it on top of a packing-case.

'If you stand to one side,' he observed, 'you do get a better idea of possible lettering on that inscription. I wonder if the glass plate itself . . .'

Bronwen opened the box in which her most recent plates had been secured. She set the one of the chancel down in the light; and handed Caspian a magnifying-glass. He stooped, edging his way round the packing-case and tilting the glass at experimental angles. Then, abruptly, he stopped and was utterly still.

'Yes. My God. I believe one can read it. But there must be a mistake.'

She stood beside him, took the glass, and positioned herself as his guiding hand instructed.

In some odd way the thickness of the glass plate added a new dimension to the flat picture, as if the lettering were etched into it as it had been etched into the stone. Moving an inch this way and an inch that way, to get different textures of light through the letters, Bronwen picked them out slowly and out of order. After she had established the main words, the blanks seemed to fill themselves in of their own accord.

Pray f— deliv-rance fr— . . .

She narrowed her eyes. Letting the picture go ever so slightly out of focus, one got a clearer sense of what the lines must be.

And the sense, unless they had both misread the inscription, was a distressing one.

Pray for deliverance from
Matilda
who did leave piouf feclufion
to feek worldlie gratification
but waf thruft back in
for her own good.

'That can't be right,' said Bronwen. 'It must surely be "Pray for deliverance *for* Matilda".'

Caspian leaned again over the picture. 'No. The word is there: "*from* Matilda".'

'But why?' Bronwen was writing the full text out on a sheet of paper. When she came to the end, she shivered. The awfulness of it: *thrust back in for her own good.*

What had that poor, long-dead creature done?

'I think,' said Caspian quietly, 'that just to set our own minds at rest, we will after all deliver the pictures to Ladygrove Manor on our homeward journey.'

That night Bronwen was snared in a cruel, confused dream. Trying to fight her way out of a suffocating cupboard which at one moment was in a corner of the Caernarvon house, at another somehow transported to the heart of Ladygrove maze, she was pushed back over and over again. Gasping for breath, she tried to set her shoulder against the door as it closed for what she was sure would be the last time. Then a hand stole over her shoulder and around her back, and she woke up moaning to find Caspian turning her gently, insistently towards him. He soothed her, murmured her into drowsy contentment; and while she was still half-asleep he came gently and lovingly into her, and she dreamily responded and then slept, fulfilled and well pleased.

They had telegraphed their time of arrival to David, and the trap was waiting at the station, driven by a groom who explained that Sir David had been called away to a small fire in one of the barns. Last time they had made this journey, it was to the sound of their friend's enthusiasm. Now they travelled the circuitous route over a ridge, down along a side of the valley and at last into Mockblane and over the bridge, in near silence, not wanting to say anything which the man might pick up and pass on to the other servants; and, as they drew closer to Ladygrove, having nothing else they wished to talk about.

At the door Judith was waiting, just as on that last arrival. But she had changed. At first glance Bronwen could not determine where the change lay: she was perhaps a trifle haggard, yet at the same time showed a certain inner complacency – which might have been accounted for by the child within her, but somehow was not.

'David will be back as soon as he can. He'll be so pleased to see you again – and the pictures. They've been successful, have they?'

She led the way into the hall.

Bronwen and Caspian followed, and stopped dead in the centre of the polished floor.

What had happened?

Their minds reached for each other.

'You managed to settle everything in Caernarvon?' Judith was asking.

The house is worse. The house, everything. Much, much worse than before.

✣ 2 ✣

'I want a daughter,' declared Judith, 'not a son. And not born in this house.'

Margaret nodded a vigorous, no-nonsense nod. Herself the mother of one girl and one boy, she was briskly certain that the order of birth mattered nothing and that averages would probably work out as tidily for all normal people as they had done for her.

'Whichever it is,' she said breezily, 'you'll be glad to have it out so you may start thinking about the next.'

Judith managed a wan smile.

David's sister was tall and bony, her complexion leathery from years in an inimical climate, but handsome. A woman accustomed to giving orders and coping smartly with crises, she had come home to Ladygrove Manor with curling upper lip and a contrarily wide, spontaneous grin. Brusque disdain alternated with bursts of heartiness. From the moment of first meeting her sister-in-law she made it plain that for normal women having a child was perfectly normal – of no greater consequence than dropping a foal in a paddock, nudging it to its feet and licking it, and then going off for a skittish canter across the meadows.

'I don't blame you,' she conceded as the two of them sat at the open window surveying a scene which had grown wearisomely familiar to Judith, 'for wanting to be away from here for the confinement. I was thousands of miles away for mine, heaven be praised. Atmosphere of this place'd dampen anyone's spirits. Can't think why you let yourself be dragged here.'

'David had to take over the estate.'

'Shouldn't have let him. Do you no good, no good at all. Put a bailiff in, collect the rents and invest the profits, live where you choose to live.'

'David loves it here. He has always wanted to come back.'

'Only because he didn't have to spend all his time here when he was young. Not like me. Fine for him, coming home from school for the holidays and being spoilt – the young master, y'know – and then off to study, and then off to London, and back again when it suited him. I had them – father and mother, I had them – day in, day out. Unhealthy place this, always was.'

Margaret got up and glared out of the window with the ferocity of a colonial administrator, arms akimbo and bony hips askew.

Judith said: 'David will never want to leave here. It wouldn't be fair to ask him.'

'You'd be glad to see the back of it though, wouldn't you?'

'I . . . I'd like to be away when the baby's born.'

'So you shall be. Tell him.'

'He has promised.'

'Make sure he keeps to it.' Margaret's sisterly scorn was a tart, invigorating tonic. Then she stooped and looked out, hunching one shoulder up. 'Here come those friends of yours.' The mere word 'friends' conveyed a judgment on two inexplicable, unreliable eccentrics.

Bronwen and Alexander Caspian came round the end of the terrace, she with a bulkier camera than she had used last time, he carrying a plate box as before. They glanced up and Bronwen waved, slowing in the hope that Judith would join them.

She hesitated.

'Better keep an eye on them,' said Margaret in cheerful mistrust.

Judith was surprised by her own uncertainty. When Bronwen and Caspian had gone away she had longed for them to come back – and soon. Now that they were here they did not seem such close friends as they had once been. That close communion she had once admired now seemed sly, secretive, insultingly unforthcoming. But here they were; and it was she and David who had invited them. She went down on to the grass.

'We were wondering,' said Bronwen, 'whether the footbridge has been repaired yet.'

'It has, yes. Everything's perfectly normal again.'

'Then perhaps I can get inside this time.' Bronwen added, as if the answer were of no consequence: 'When you say perfectly normal does that mean you've overcome the other troubles as well?'

'Oh, those silly vapours of mine?' Judith was reluctant to tell too much, and even in herself not sure precisely what there was to tell. 'Truly, I can't account for those. So silly.'

'You mean you can go in and out as you please?'

'As I please, yes.'

'Whatever are we talking about?' Margaret was almost as tall and imposing as Caspian. Until she had reached a secure judgment on him she set herself against him, chin raised, at her full challenging height.

He smiled courteously at her, but addressed Judith. 'Bronwen won't be satisfied until she has taken some pictures of the interior.'

'There's so little to see. Nothing of any real importance.'

Again there was an unspoken question as the two consulted each other in that strange way of theirs. Judith reluctantly supposed she must escort them into the maze to demonstrate how innocuous it was. They would not be in there for long, and it would mean nothing to them: a picture or two and they would go away, and she would be left to enjoy it in peace.

Until David took her to London. In London they would meet again and she would see them differently. Everything would be different in London. It was just this place that put things in the wrong perspective. Perspective . . . one of David's favourite words.

She must have a girl and escape the malediction, so that there should be no strife betwixt her and David.

Judith led them down the slope and unfalteringly over the bridge.

In the maze she took no wrong turning. Smoothly she let herself be steered this way and that, deflected and guided and accustomed to each step so that she would soon be able to do it in her sleep. The others trod behind her, not exchanging a word.

She began to sympathize with Lady Brobury. It was essential to have somewhere private and personal, some secluded corner in which to shut oneself away from people, even one's friends.

Sunlight warmed the cold stones of the anchoress's cell. Inside it remained cold, but was musty no longer, no longer as she had first encountered it. The floor was swept, revealing not the packed earthen floor she had first expected but a single smooth stone slab, its surface broken only by a scattering of twigs.

Surprise pricked at her mind. And although she had not spoken, Bronwen responded involuntarily: 'What is it?'

The twigs, said Judith. But she did not say it aloud. Looking down expressionlessly at the pattern of rowan, oak and ash laid out on the stone, she knew it had been altered since she was here yesterday; and knew that even if she had understood the reason she would not have wanted to talk about it.

Bronwen set up her camera and took pictures of the exterior. Light within was too uncertain for a satisfactory study of the cell's interior. Then there were a couple of pictures of a corner of the maze, and one of a junction of three deceptive paths. Margaret watched the procedure with a superciliousness which would have done credit to her mother.

Shepherding them out of the maze, Judith paused at the exit and looked back. She felt an impulse to go in and sit down, on her own, in silence. Walking there and back in their company had tired her unreasonably.

Margaret said sharply: 'My dear Judith, what's troubling you?'

'I'm a little fatigued. I suppose I must have done too much this morning.'

'Nonsense. You've done hardly anything this morning. Really, this place is having the most deplorable effect on you.'

Caspian offered Judith his arm. She hesitated fractionally, then accepted it. Margaret tried to walk alongside, but every few seconds showed a tendency to stalk impatiently ahead.

The Dowager Lady Brobury was waiting for them.

It seemed to Judith that her mother-in-law was always watching over her nowadays – not flutteringly and volubly, as she had been a few weeks earlier, but calmly, waiting patiently, setting herself unassumingly back from the scene yet always a part of it.

Margaret marched up to her mother. 'I've a good mind to take Judith with me to Hereford.'

'Whatever for?'

'Until David condescends to arrange things for her in London.'

'You're so impulsive, Margaret. I had hoped you'd have grown out of such things.'

'It will do her good.'

'It's out of the question.'

'What do you mean, mother – out of the question? If Judith wants to get away –'

'*Does* Judith want to get away?'

They were all looking at her. Judith wanted to shout yes, of course she wanted to get away, she *must* get away . . . David must take her. David would take her.

'When David's ready,' she said.

Lady Brobury nodded. 'Still trampling your way through other folk's plans,' she said to her daughter.

'I still think it would do Judith a world of good to have a rest.'

'She may rest where and how she chooses.' Lady Brobury bestowed a bland smile on the group and turned away, disappearing unhurriedly into the house.

She was hardly out of earshot when Margaret said: 'Something's happened to mother. She is so direct. So sure of herself.'

'She's getting over the shock of –'

'Of father's death? Oh, there's more to it than that. She used to be such a fuss, forever dabbing and dabbling and then dodging away. Now she looks so smug. As if she knew something the rest of us don't. And I don't care for it.'

Judith had to laugh. Margaret's indignation was so direct and explosive, brooking no nuances or half-measures.

'She always *wanted* to be in the centre of things,' Margaret went on, 'but father talked her down, and went against her wishes in running the house or . . . oh, in anything at all. And she never had quite the right manner to impress the villagers or the farmers, so she couldn't get any satisfaction from playing Lady Bountiful. Poor mother – I always felt she had missed something and didn't even know what it was she had missed. But now she has the air of having found something. I'm not at all sure it's good for her.'

'You make it sound as if she's taking the wrong sort of medicine.'

'Depending on the ailment, that's rather a . . .'

Margaret's voice trailed away. It had occurred to her that the Caspians were still close at hand. Her lips tightened. Family matters were not for discussion in front of strangers.

Bronwen tapped the edge of the plate box her husband was carrying. 'When we've put all this away, perhaps we could stroll over to the village and deliver Mr Goswell's prints.'

On the bridge they stopped for a moment. It commanded a view to one side of Ladygrove Manor, to the other of the village. The contrast in the colours of church and cottages had been wiped out by the growing sullenness of the sky, and even the water below the bridge lacked its usual sparkle. Shadow touched the idyllic scene which Bronwen had carried away in her memory.

She said: 'What do you make of the situation now?'

'I agree with Mrs Henderson. Something has happened to her mother.'

'To the whole house. And to Judith – or is beginning to happen to her.'

'Mrs Henderson notices it only in her mother.'

'Since we were last here . . .' Bronwen groped for a way of expressing it, then gave up the struggle. Her thoughts were Caspian's thoughts, her questions his.

He said: 'Something was driven out. And something else, something worse, is filling up the vacuum.'

They went on their way.

The Reverend Frederick Goswell was effusively delighted to see them. He offered chairs in the window overlooking his garden and the churchyard beyond, and stood above them accepting one print at a time, bobbing his head in appreciation, and setting each one carefully on a side table when he had finished with it.

'Excellent. Most commendable. I envy you your skill, Mrs Caspian.'

They saved the picture of the inscription until last.

Now his head shook instead of nodding. 'Ah, what a pity. But one could expect little else, could one? In a few months' time, perhaps, if we can find a mason with sufficient skill to clean out the lettering, we may be able to interpret it.'

'With the aid of the original plate and a magnifying-glass,' said Caspian, 'we have reached an interpretation.'

'The wonders of modern science! I can scarcely credit it.'

Caspian laid on top of the neat pile of prints a sheet written in his fine, regular hand. The vicar read it; mouthed a few words over again; and jerked his head back in protest. 'But this is not possible.'

'We can see no other reading.'

'Praying for deliverance *from* Matilda? Really, Dr Caspian, your eyes have deceived you. Obviously the inscription enjoins us to pray for the soul of the revered Matilda – a quite common form of wording.'

'That was my own first thought. But my wife has also studied the inscription most painstakingly, and is equally convinced.'

'And "thrust back in for her own good".' Mr Goswell's head shook ever more vigorously. 'This is deplorable. Why should a young woman of such known holiness be reviled in such a manner?'

'Why was the plaque set in your chancel in the first place?'

'I have no records of its installation, but the concept is natural enough. When the old site by Ladygrove Manor was taken over and this new church built, it was surely in reverence and affection that the memory of Matilda of Mockblane should be recalled here, too. Later apostates may have tried to obliterate that sacred memory, but the original intention can hardly be doubted.'

'To guard *against* Matilda's lingering influence?'

'I will not hear it. There is some error somewhere. Whatever other unhappy spirits may have plagued these parts . . .' He stopped.

'There have been spirits, then?' said Caspian crisply. 'Manifestations? Revenants?'

'The sins of the fathers –'

'What did you do' – the revelation blazed suddenly in Caspian's mind, and Bronwen felt it burning through to her – 'in Ladygrove Manor?'

'I?'

'Yes, you, vicar. What did you drive out?'

'I don't know what right you have to ask me this.'

'So you did meddle.'

84

'That is a most offensive word, Dr Caspian. I did no more than my duty.'

'To whom?'

'To the family which has been generous enough to appoint me to this living. They were distressed, there was undoubtedly a disruptive force within that house; and I am thankful that it was in my power to drive it out, as you put it.'

'You mean you – '

'I performed a holy rite of exorcism, yes,' said Mr Goswell proudly.

Caspian's dark beard seemed to thicken and flow inwards, intruding its darkness on his cheeks, which flushed deeper and deeper with anger.

'Do you know the damage you may have done, dabbling – '

'Sir! I will not accept these insults from you. I do not meddle, or dabble. I am the humble instrument of the Lord.'

'You have done some terrible damage.' Caspian's voice shook, until Bronwen sent out a plea that he should control his temper. More evenly he managed to continue: 'Something in Ladygrove Manor is even more disturbing than anything which afflicted it before. My wife and I both recognized this the very moment we returned.'

'And what are your qualifications for such a judgment, Dr Caspian?'

'My husband' – Bronwen spoke for him – 'has devoted his life to the study of occult dangers – '

'And has the impertinence to call *me* a dabbler?'

Caspian had his temper well under control by now. 'Let us suppose, vicar, that in all good faith you drove out a spirit from that house, only to learn now that it may have been a benevolent spirit rather than an evil one?'

'A benevolent phantom is a contradiction in terms.'

'There are no distinctions? No possibility of emanations of living people's fears or wishes, so that a psychical power for good – '

'Whatever continues to roam this vale of tears after death,' said Mr Goswell staunchly, 'must by definition be accursed. If there is to be any hope of salvation for it, then for its own wretched sake as well as for that of others it must be driven from this earthly plane.

85

'I'm puzzled,' he admitted, 'that no previous incumbent thought to exorcize it.'

'Or thought of it, and then thought better of it?'

'It may be,' Mr Goswell went on with modest pride, 'that earlier attempts failed from lack of faith. I was granted a stronger power. I do assure you that I felt a very positive force beside me, adding its strength to mine and guiding me.'

'Who else was with you,' asked Bronwen, 'at the time of this ceremony?'

'Lady Brobury. That is, ah, both of them: Lady Brobury and the Dowager Lady Brobury, of course.'

'It seems odd that the elder Lady Brobury should have participated in an exorcism designed to drive out the very Matilda of whom she has made her own private cult.'

'I do not accept that it was the blessed Matilda. Nor do I accept your translation of that inscription. Whatever it was that infested Ladygrove Manor, it was something which came between Lady Brobury and her devotions. Now the obstruction has been removed.'

The finality in his manner suggested that the whole matter was now closed. He owed nobody any explanation or justification.

As they rose to go, Caspian fired one snap shot. 'This was all done with Sir David's approval, I presume?'

The vicar remained stiffly erect, uncommunicative.

'I see,' said Caspian softly. 'You performed the rite in his house without his knowing.'

'Lady Brobury, a good and God-fearing lady with the interests of her entire family at heart – '

'Who persuaded you to act without her son's knowledge.'

'We did not discuss the matter on any such terms.'

'But Sir David,' Caspian persisted, 'was not present.'

'I believe he had been called away at the last minute to visit his sister in Hereford.'

'Ah, I see.'

'Whatever you think you see, Dr Caspian, I shall be grateful if you will not distort it for the benefit of others – as you have distorted the dedication to Matilda of Mockblane.' With an effort, as they reached the door, Mr Goswell said: 'I am grateful to you for the donation of photographs. I shall study them keenly.'

'It would be well for you to do so,' was Caspian's parting fling.

Bronwen felt the aimless anger within him as they walked away, and reached mentally for him, trying to soothe the turmoil.

'Perhaps we're exaggerating the damage he may have done,' she said. 'After all, if ever there was a beneficent spirit, or some lingering psychic force for good, it didn't perform all that efficiently in the past. By all accounts it gave little comfort to many of the earlier Broburys.'

'You're thinking of the strife between man and wife? But the fulfilment of that curse may still have been preferable to the alternative.'

'The "giving back"? You think that *that*'s what was being guarded against?'

'I don't know if there ever was a guardian, or ever was anything to guard against. How much is the accumulation of family tradition and superstition, and how much of a lasting resonance there may be, creating inner discord and strife for those susceptible to it – no, I don't know.'

'But you're worried.'

'As you were a little while ago, for Judith.'

'You think she's in worse danger?'

'I think that Lady Brobury and that clumsy, conceited fellow back there are bound to have an unhealthy effect on Judith in her present state.'

They were in shadow now, climbing the hill to the gates. Ladygrove Manor loomed darkly against the dark hillside.

The open gates provoked a vision in Bronwen's mind of another entrance – a pathway once invisibly closed to Judith, and now open. Wherever that path led, into and in some way beyond the cell at the heart of the maze, it now offered no obstacle. The worst, thought Bronwen with an acute pang of unreasoning fear, was now attainable.

Caspian glanced at her as they passed the lodge. 'We can't stay here indefinitely. And we have no authority to intervene.'

'If only that woman Margaret will do what she says, and take Judith away.'

'Away from what?'

'From whatever it is,' said Bronwen, 'that's being wished on her.'

As if in answer to her prayer, David and his sister were crossing the hall as they entered, and the tone of Margaret's harangue left little doubt as to the course of argument so far.

'All very fine,' Margaret was holding forth. 'You're inundated with work. I quite understand that. Father was never too assiduous in managing the estate, and I can imagine there's a great deal to be put right. Any wife with any character at all knows that, stands by the man. Doesn't make herself a nuisance. But she can happily be a nuisance to *me*. Save that she wouldn't be a nuisance at all.'

'Meg, I've told you a dozen times already, the moment I can take Judith away – '

'You're not listening. As bad as father, sometimes. *I* am telling *you* that I think it will do Judith good to get away now, not when it suits you. She can come to Hereford. The house is in good shape, George won't be home on leave for six weeks yet, and I'm not used to sitting about on my own for that many weeks on end. So you will be doing me a favour by letting Judith come. I've told Judith the same.'

Bronwen began to feel a liking for Margaret Henderson. For all her overbearing manner she was, if not subtle in getting her own way, at least generous, making other people's eventual surrender easy for them, even desirable.

David grinned, and slapped his sister's shoulder. 'If you've talked Judith into it – '

'That's settled, then.'

At dinner, Judith and her mother-in-law ate in silence while plans were made all around them: Judith apparently dazed, Lady Brobury sullen but unprotesting. David gave orders that the carriage should be ready at eight o'clock next morning, Margaret said that as soon as the meal was ended Judith must set her maid to packing everything she would need, and Caspian said really, they must be going, too. David was discussing the day when he was likely to reach Hereford himself, to collect Judith and escort her on to London; and then, belatedly registering Caspian's remark, he said:

'But there's no need for you to leave yet. Stay on a few days and come riding – give us a chance to talk.'

Lady Brobury looked up from her plate with cool, malicious

pleasure. 'You have so little time for your wife that you'll let her be bundled away from home, but you want others to stay on and entertain you.'

'Mother, that's a gross distortion.'

'We really must be on our way,' Caspian repeated tactfully.

Bronwen saw the corners of Judith's eyes pucker with a twinge of what might have been pain or puzzlement. Impulsively she said: 'Wouldn't it make things easy for everyone if we joined you in the carriage to Hereford? It would save two journeys: instead of taking that long way round to the branch line station, we could chat with Judith all the way to Hereford and find ourselves a faster train from there. Only if it suits you, of course.'

She had half expected Margaret to jib at this. Instead there came a quick glance of acceptance, welcoming her as an ally. 'Excellent idea, Mrs Caspian. What a pleasant little party it'll make! We'll be the ones with a chance to talk, and I daresay we'll make a better fist of it than David would. So that's agreed.'

'We must pack,' said Bronwen. 'Eight o'clock in the morning – that's it, isn't it?'

Judith at last smiled. The idea was slowly taking her fancy. But when she turned towards Lady Brobury the smile faded back into uncertainty. 'I do think it would be rather a nice idea, don't you, mother?'

'Oh, nobody consults me nowadays,' said Lady Brobury with unaccustomed placidity.

In the morning Caspian and Bronwen were awake early, but when they reached the breakfast salvers and tureens laid out on the sideboard it was to find Margaret already there, embarking on a hearty meal. As they helped themselves and went to the table, Judith came in, and a moment later Lady Brobury joined them, presumably to make her farewells here rather than at her lodge gate.

'You must come over and spend some time with us, mother, before Judith leaves for London,' said Margaret. Then she took a second look.

Lady Brobury was no longer in mourning. In its place she had chosen a white lace cap stiffened with threads of green and purple beads, and over a dark green dress wore a velvet-trimmed mantlet. She was very bright and wide awake.

Judith's cheeks had more colour in them this morning. She must, Bronwen surmised, have willed herself overnight into the mood for going away and enjoying the change of scene, throwing off the insidious malaise of Ladygrove Manor.

David appeared suddenly in the doorway with one fist clenched, thwacking angrily against his hip.

'The carriage,' he raged. 'How the devil could Crampton not have noticed?

Margaret's fork was poised, ready to jab. 'Noticed what?'

'That one of the wheels was near collapse. There's a crack right through the felloe, and the spokes are working loose. Gave way as soon as we tried to bring it out a few minutes ago. Damned great gash, I don't see *how* it could have gone unnoticed. Must have been dangerous for a week or more. Someone might easily have been killed.'

Normally his mother would have been the first to raise a wail of recrimination, building the mishap up to the dimensions of a tragedy which would throw out all her personal plans and calculations for months to come. Now she shrugged and helped herself lavishly to kidneys and bacon.

'You mean we can't get away on time?' There was a rasp of suspicion in Margaret's voice.

'I'm told the village wheelwright is away in Leominster for a family wedding. Not due back until the day after tomorrow, and heaven knows what condition he'll be in for a day or two after that.'

'And Judith certainly can't go any distance in the trap,' said Margaret.

Lady Brobury settled herself comfortably at the table beside Judith. 'So that's an end to *that* nonsense,' she said blandly.

3

The mare paced nervously and tossed her head as Margaret put a foot in the stirrup. Then she was steadied by the firm, confident hand on her neck.

'You always were an impatient child,' said Lady Brobury. 'Why you must rush off in this deplorable fashion I really cannot understand.'

Margaret settled herself in the saddle. 'I don't care to leave the children any longer without a visit to see how they're settling in. But' – she stared commandingly down at Judith – 'I shall have the house ready for you, and be back with my own carriage, in two days. Three at most. No more accidents, I'll see to that. And you'll not talk yourself out of it while my back's turned. David, I expect you to keep her up to it.'

'Yes, ma'am.' David favoured his sister with a mock bow.

'There's bound to be a train from Lenhale in mid-morning. And I'll enjoy the ride – years since I took this route. If I leave Jenny at the ostler's, one of the grooms can fetch her when it's convenient. All right, David?'

Lady Brobury tried again. 'I fail to see why you should not all go together in the trap. If Dr and Mrs Caspian also wish to be taken to Lenhale station – '

'In the first place,' said Margaret, 'the trap is too small for all of us, especially with Dr and Mrs Caspian's impedimenta. And in the second place I am in a hurry.'

'Just as I said. Always in a hurry, always so impetuous.'

'Remember what I said, David. Have her ready for me. And her baggage and mine.'

They waved as Margaret cantered off on to the path past the stables, up the hill and over the ridge.

'My father's favourite ride to Lenhale,' said David reminiscently. 'After all this time Jenny must know every inch of the way.'

Lady Brobury turned and went off towards her lodge without another word, save for a tetchy little exclamation as Pippin bounded past her, narrowly failing to knock her over. He sniffed at Judith's feet, raised his head, and began to run in the direction Margaret had taken.

'Pippin, come back,' shouted David.

'Pippin.' Judith's voice was more coaxing. But the dog, who had recently spent so much time in her company, now ignored her altogether and went racing on up the slope. 'Pippin, good boy, Pippin!'

'He'll soon tire,' said David.

Judith watched until the sleek golden shape was out of sight, then went indoors. She looked deflated: brought to the pitch of going away and sharing other company for a while, she now faced a day as predictable as any other.

'If we're to make a reasonable train connection,' said Caspian, 'I think we had better load the trap and set off.'

David's gaze had been following his wife. Now he turned back to his guests. 'I was hoping you'd stay.'

'But everything is packed, I thought we – '

'Please.' He spoke in a low, urgent tone. 'Margaret is right. We must get Judith away, and I must make the effort to join her as soon as possible. I'll get through as much as I can in the next few days. I've got to be sure of the contracts for taking the harvest – and there's the harvesters' brewer and baker to be seen to. But if you could be here until ... well, until Margaret gets back. Would you?' He hesitated, then added: 'To come between mother and Judith.'

'Between them?'

'I'm sure it's not mother's fault, but I do see what Margaret sees – that she's having a bad effect on Judith. Making every allowance, I still wish she could be less ... oh, the devil take it, I don't even begin to know what's perplexing me.'

'Making allowances for crotchety old relatives,' said Bronwen, 'can be overdone, making due allowance for the fact that they are so often in the wrong.'

'I'm not saying mother's in the wrong. Simply that in some way she's an unfortunate influence. I'd be much relieved if you could spend some time with Judith, and try . . .'

'Yes?'

David looked full at Caspian. 'I've told you that I don't know. Don't begin to know. And I don't know how to ask this. But all that occult knowledge of yours, the way you practised mesmerism on that disturbed child in London, and what I've heard about you bringing peace to what seemed to be two cases of demoniacal possession . . . Not that I believe in ghosts as such, or possession, or – '

'Or family curses?' suggested Caspian gently.

David groaned. 'Oh, very well. I've got to come out with it, haven't I?'

'It will do little good to suppress it.'

'There's something wrong. Or, at least, something not quite right. It means nothing to me, and I'd sooner not listen. But it's throwing everything off balance, and if you do have these special powers which would help – help Judith above all – I'd appreciate your taking an interest. I don't mean to trespass too much on your time, but . . .'

Bronwen and Caspian had no need to look at each other. It was with their mutual assent that Caspian said: 'Of course we'll stay.'

'Alex. Bronwen. If *you* will keep an eye on Judith, in whichever way you think is best . . .'

'We'll keep an eye on Judith.'

For the next hour-and-a-half there was no call for them to undertake this function. David, refuting his mother's barbed accusation of the evening before, postponed his departure for the day's routine and strolled in the grounds with his wife. Even from a distance one could see – Bronwen and Caspian could see – that she was restless. For a few minutes she would take his arm and then shrug away. He talked more assiduously than usual and she listened fitfully, looking away most of the time. The anticlimax dragged her down: after such a flurry of preparation for leaving Ladygrove, here she was sinking back into the Ladygrove atmosphere.

In the middle of the morning David made an excuse to leave her. He wanted to give further consideration to the damaged carriage wheel. Left to her own devices, Judith continued to saunter round the garden with the air of one who had been given no instruction to do otherwise. Her own momentum carried her on slowly and automatically until some impulse nudged her into another direction.

Down the slope she went at the same pace, across the bridge and towards the maze beyond.

Caspian and Bronwen tensed. They had stationed themselves, mentally quiescent, in the coign of a mullioned window: watching without spying, keeping an eye on Judith according to David's plea – 'in whichever way you think is best'. They had not intruded; but now they were alert. Adjusted to her rhythm of thought and movement, they sensed the change of tempo.

They walked casually to the edge of the lawn as she disappeared, an infinity below, into the grove.

'If we're to help,' said Caspian in little more than a whisper, 'we must follow her in.'

'She may not want our company.'

'She is not to know that she has it.'

They went swiftly but unobtrusively to the fringe of the grove and found themselves a sheltered patch within a clump of bushes, shielded from the house and from the entrance to the maze. The house was in any case meaningless now. But they saw the opening into the maze clearly enough, and the trickery of the hedges within: saw it all through Judith's languid eyes.

Caspian propped his shoulder against his wife's and let his muscles go slack. Bronwen's weight adjusted to his. They let their minds mesh; and let them float in a gossamer net over and around Judith, so lightly that she was aware of no contact, while they were aware of every tremor.

She was still half in a trance of boredom, letting herself tread unseeking through the yew avenues. She did not know why she had come here; but did not know why she might better be anywhere else.

Then slowly, shifting, like the blackness of a silhouette blurring and fading and then intensifying into a new shape on a shadow-play screen, she was Judith no longer. She surrendered her consciousness to things she would not, later, remember.

94

The Caspians drifted with her on the swell of the past, beating soundlessly in through the sluice of the present. But there was no present, never had been and never could be: the present was, is and shall be only an infinitesimal instant, a watershed where the past accumulates in order to erode the future.

They were in Judith and in that other for minutes only, yet those minutes were simultaneously hours and months and years, and had endured for centuries. Pain and desire were immediate but eternal; ephemeral but undying.

I am here, I offer myself humbly, I beg for deliverance from the world. The ills of the world shall be set behind me. Grant me this, and my prayers for the sufferers shall not cease.

There shall be no temptation and no falsehood. This shall be made a holy place, a rock of sanctity firm in the swamps of wickedness. I pray for it to become so.

And so it shall be. The cell is consecrated and I have been prepared for it. I am shriven, and shall be protected from further sin. The bishop himself says the office and places his own seal on the last stone to be set in place. Prayers are said within and without the church, and psalms chanted below my single slit of a window. And if I – perhaps I alone – hear the laughter foul and destructive below the prayers and singing, I fear not. Let them laugh and blaspheme, those who shun truth and cling to error. I will not be afraid. They will not relinquish the old ways and the old demons. Still they will practise the older abominations in the older places in the hills, and the secret places of this accursed valley. But I will fear not, they shall have no power over me. With my prayers and with God's help they shall be cast out.

The entrance is sealed, the words have been said, they have all devoutly gone and left me to my devotions. There is silence outside, and blessed silence within.

Dicamus omnes, Domine, miserere.

I am alone but not alone. How can there be loneliness where there is perfect love and perfect peace?

The stone of the floor is cold. The walls are cold. Day and night, all is cold. I wake and pray, and am cold. But I am warmed by love and sustained by love, by the adoration and the needs of all those who come to breathe and murmur against the outward walls.

'Pray for us, Matilda. For my daughter who is sick with a fever, and for my son taken in the covert by the king's warrener.'

I will pray for you.

'Pray for us on this our wedding day . . .'

I will pray.

'Blessed Matilda, intercede for my erring child . . .'

'We bring thanks for prayers answered . . .'

Deo gratias.

They bring alms. They bring food and gifts, and I hear them being placed outside my cell. Then comes the priest to decide which food shall be laid within the slit of window, and which shall be apportioned between his and the bishop's households.

What does it taste like, the food they take away from my offerings?

Pray for their souls.

I have sinned. I have thought with envy of meats and bread, I have coveted that which was offered not to me but to the greater glory of God.

Deus, miserere. Deus, miserere.

I shall not think of the world. All I see of it is not truly this world but the sign of the next. Through my squint I take part in the Mass, seen by none and seeing only the celebrant at the high altar.

Nor do I wish to see more.

But I wonder if my sisters are in the church, and if they chattered on the way here and will chatter just as ever on their way down the valley? If either is yet to be wed. And if my brother is there.

Where sits the knave who seduced the wretched wight Anne, cottar's daughter from the white brook? I have answered the pleas of the goodwife and prayed for the girl, and will pray for the man also that he may be redeemed, and will think ill of none. But what sports do they play, these knaves, in wilful despite of the damnation which they must know awaits them?

I would curse them, the proud, the wicked, the wanton.

But it is not for me to curse but to ask forgiveness.

And is the daughter of Goodman Peter at Mass, planning another offering to be set outside my cell, that I may offer up prayers for her fertility? How shall I, without unchaste thoughts, ask that she be blessed with child?

It was from such demands, such shames, that I fled. From such ignominy I have shut myself away.

I bow my head to the cold stone floor to cool my errant thoughts. But the floor has grown warm. I feel the beat of a heart within it and I think of the heart which shall begin to beat as the girl swells with her child, and if I allow myself to touch myself I can believe that I too . . .

No. It shall not be. These are blasphemous thoughts. They are not mine. I repudiate them.

I am free of worldly desire. I will speak for others but not for myself.

Hear my plea. For this old woman in pain. For this man in torment. For shepherd and farrier, for master and vassal. For swineherd . . .

There! There is the laughter again, the same laughter. It is louder now, and no longer outside, but here in the cell with me: below me, making the very floor shake with foul mirth.

What are these dreams throbbing up from the floor and into my head, my limbs, into every aching secret place of my body?

I am too hot. I have been ill. It may be that food placed on my ledge carried a plague, that there will be pestilence through the village and the valley and through me. Yesterday I was in prayer when the world went dark and the floor began to burn. Yesterday – or a sennight since?

Time passes. No, there is no time. It is all one to me: day, night, voices of the faithful outside and in, the chanting of psalms in the church and the laughter of these other voices within my head.

This is no holy place. It was but is no longer. I bring shame upon it.

Wicked visions do sorely torment my mind and flesh.

Here is someone at night, come to whisper a plea to me through the wall. There are many of them like this, finding it easier to ask for prayers under cover of darkness than to speak when the priest might pass and overhear. Like this? No, not like this one. He brings temptation, not piety: talks of the spring flowers, the smell of the woodlands, the sound of the river and of children's voices, and of dancing and bestial good cheer.

Or is it a voice within these walls – within myself?

I have begged the priest to bring a birch that I may flagellate myself.

It does but make me the hotter.

I am not worthy to be here, I shall bring an abomination upon this place. I am letting in demons.

Or have the demons been here for untold centuries, waiting for me?

I must be sent out from here. I cannot endure. I am wretched and infirm, help Thou mine infirmities. I ask to be taken back into the wicked world, for my wickedness is too great for aught else.

Yes, father, I do so renounce my vows. Yes, my lord bishop, this I do truly intend.

Vah, perii, nihil est reliqui mihi, cur esse coepi?

They are waiting outside, so many of them. It might be a market day, or the day of a fair, and I am to be the buffoon, the travelling juggler, the minstrel who will entertain them. The stones are chipped out to make an opening large enough for me to step through, and there is a murmur when I am free and standing on the grass.

It is true that the grass smells sweet.

Mercifully the day is masked by cloud, but still it is too bright for my eyes. When I lower them I am aware of the other eyes devouring me; but when I try to look up and meet those other eyes, I am faint with the vastness of sky and hill and valley. If I reach out there are no safely enclosing walls to touch.

A man stumbles forward and kneels and would kiss my hand. He is trying to thank me for some prayer I offered on his behalf, but he is too close, and there is no wall between us, and I would run if there were anywhere I might run.

Others grin, and speak behind their hands. They have come to enjoy the spectacle and will talk about it afterwards and laugh about it.

Already there is laughter.

I must escape.

My father is not here, my brother and sisters are not in the throng.

They have shunned it. It may be that they will wish to disown me. It is no small thing to have a holy woman in the family, the object of devotion and the interpreter of prayers. It is a very poor thing to have a useless daughter returning to become a burden on the household.

Yet I have nowhere else to go.

One man was still grateful and knelt to me. Now an old woman sinks unsteadily to her knees and raises her arms to me. But another woman snarls like an animal, and a man spits. I have betrayed them. If I have shown so little faith, how shall they keep theirs? The cell is open and empty. I am deserting them.

'Matilda, if you would spend some time with an order of sisters of charity, I promise you a welcome . . .'

The bishop is stern but kind, but knows nothing of stone floors and what may rise from them, or of what may ensnare a mind shut away within stone walls. My fortress had become a prison. I could not commit myself to another.

So I must run.

They call after me as I begin to hurry away from the cell and the church, running away from them towards the hillside. Some are calling me back, wishing kindness on me. Others scream imprecations. And four of the men set out after me, as they would pursue a runaway bitch.

I am weak, I have not walked for so long that I have no strength for a chase.

Now the bishop and priest call them back. They deem it safer to let me run wild than let their pack sink their teeth into me.

Where shall I flee? There is nobody now in the vale to shelter me, unless I recant and pretend to be once more what I never could be. But there are those in the hills who may accept me.

Where did I learn that, who spoke of it to me?

'Well, young wench, what seek you?'

It is a young man's voice, and the voice of a man of good position, sure of himself. I glimpse only the arrogant set of him, leaning against a tree in the shade of dancing leaves, one foot advanced towards me as if proposing we should both join the dance.

My ragged woollen habit, coarse against my skin as I had once wished it to be, makes a fool of me out in this alien world. There is too much space, men can see too far and too much. I cross my arms across my breast and roll face down on the earth, and smell earth and grass and cannot but moan at the joy of it. Let the man but go away and leave me to this moment, so that breath and reason can be restored to me.

'Upon my soul, how you do stink.' This is the laughter I have feared, and a laughter of such vigour that I have other reasons to fear it. I would turn my head to steal a glance, but dare not. 'Yet it's a woman's stink, for all that.' A foot prods mockingly into my ribs. 'I have known worse.'

There comes a ruder jab. I pull awake like the abject, crawling animal it is my fate to be, still shielding my face for I know it to be grimed and unkempt and fit only to provoke greater mockery from such a man.

'Let me look on you, mistress.'

'Sir, I beg you. I wish to go my way. I seek only solitude and seclusion.'

'You have had your share of solitude, little virgin, and found it little to your taste. So I have heard. Now you seek something other.'

'I seek only to go my own way, sir.'

'Say you so? But your haunches give you the lie.' He has stamped closer and kicks again, ever more insolently. 'Would you not taste a man, my fair?'

'No!'

Fear thrusts me to my feet and fear drives me in spite of my feebleness, drives me on up the hill and along its shoulder. I can choose my path but accept that which falls most readily before me. To my right, a stone hall and wooden outbuildings. Ahead, a rise and fall of land and a wood in which I may seek refuge, and cloudy sky into which I would fain fall and be drowned. Far below, church and cell to which I must never return. Close behind, the footsteps and harsh breath of the hunter, joying in the chase.

I am burning, deliver me from this heat.

The earth rocks and rises against me. I fall, and roll twice over before tussocks of grass catch and stop me.

His hand is impatient, tearing at the poor soiled cloth, tearing it away from my poor stinking body, even before he looks into my face. When he has me pinned down and rears up to look at me, the sweat gleaming along his upper lip, he laughs and curses and then laughs again, and sweats the more.

Its lines twisting and tightening, the face is in shadow first to the left, then to the right, as he wrenches to and fro, back and forth. And then descends on me and blots out the world.

It is a face I shall not forget and not forgive, never throughout eternity.

It was the face of David Brobury.

Bronwen flinched instinctively away, and Caspian's mind reeled with hers. There was a shudder as three, four minds intermingled and then lost their grip. It was not just Matilda but Judith who looked up into those greedy eyes and then into darkness, separate yet incapable of freeing herself so abruptly.

Bronwen spun around the edge of the whirlpool and then was sucked back in. She held to Caspian, drew him with her.

Drew him into pain and terror. Yet also there was the wild laughter – the pain of the knife in the flesh, but the howl of pagan delight, the ravished girl struggling to pull away from the wound yet clinging to her ravisher and howling into his face.

Bronwen felt the agony and the frenzy within her, and it was her fingers which tore at the man upon her. Most terrifying of all, consumed by the phantom savagery of the past, she was consumed also by Matilda's answering frenzy, abandoning herself and knowing all that Matilda knew.

Then there was the disintegration, the sudden shredding away of mind and body. The man was failing, his flesh shrivelling within her. She – they – were gasping, clinging and imploring. But Caspian had deserted her, he was no longer sharing and shoring up her concentration. Out of the whirlpool he pulled away, back to the present.

It was no longer David Brobury's face but her husband's, close to hers. They were behind the copse as when they started, but instead of holding her against his shoulder he was twisted round to face her, staring with something akin to loathing in his eyes.

Bronwen swayed, and put a hand to the ground to steady herself.

'You were enjoying it.' He lashed the words at her as if to cut a weal across her face. 'You . . . you *wanted* him. It was you who gave in to him, you who lusted . . .'

Still shaken, she could not believe that they were yet fully restored to reality. She put out a hand to Caspian. 'My dearest, it was not our mind but hers. To understand, we had to suffer – '

'To suffer? For you there was no suffering, nothing but rapture. *Your* craving . . . *your* wantonness.'

It could not be true. It could not be real, any more than what they had just undergone was real.

Through the trees came the rustling, unhurried footsteps of Judith returning from the maze.

4

'Where's Pippin?' Judith had walked twice round the house, through the stableyard and a few hundred yards up the hill and down again, calling. There was no answer. The dog had been missing all day, and now that dusk was taking over the vale Judith began to grow anxious. 'He couldn't have gone all the way to Lenhale with Margaret?'

'She would hardly have taken him with her on the train,' said Caspian.

'There's no telling what either of them would do,' said Lady Brobury. 'Each as uncontrollable as the other.'

They stood within the casement window opening on to the terrace. Judith felt the cool prickling of the evening air at her throat but was somehow reluctant to turn and go indoors. She would, in any case, have had to push her way past Caspian, who had taken up a stance between her and Lady Brobury. It occurred to her that he had done this two or three times during the course of the afternoon as if, deprived of Pippin's company, she needed another faithful attendant – and one who would keep Lady Brobury at arm's length. Judith found it oddly irritating, without being quite sure what was wrong. When Caspian occasionally caught her eye, he seemed to see far too deeply into her, like a man who had once seen her in an unflattering light and now waited to catch her out once more.

Hadn't David talked of taking him riding, so that they would have a chance to talk? Yet they had not gone riding: Caspian had been close to her all afternoon, and David was nowhere to be seen.

Caspian said: 'I suppose the dog may have encountered David and gone off with him for an hour or so.'

'David has not gone far all day.' Lady Brobury was staring tranquilly down the garden. 'He is already back, but there's no dog with him.'

'David's back, and I haven't seen him?' Judith complained.

'He appears to be occupied elsewhere.'

'Not still fussing over that carriage wheel?'

Her mother-in-law tipped the faintest inclination of her head towards the edge of the lawn where the descent to the grove began. At its southern extremity, framed between uprights of the rose garden pergola, Bronwen and David were engaged in earnest conversation. In the twilight their heads were close together. Once Bronwen put a hand on David's arm. He shook his head, raised the arm in one of his sweeping gestures, and then went on shaking his head.

Within the window embrasure there was a silence more awkward than the most halting conversation.

'They seem to have a great deal to discuss,' said Lady Brobury.

Caspian moved away from the two ladies and strode down the slope, too resolutely to be casual. He stood beside his wife, yet in some way they looked farther apart than Judith had ever seen them.

'I wish I knew what had happened to Pippin,' she fretted. 'Obviously he's not down there.'

'You'd do better to concern yourself with more important things. As that Dr Caspian of yours is doing.'

'Important in what way?'

'From the look of the man, I'd say he's waking up to facts rather more quickly than you.'

'Mother, whatever are we supposed to be talking about?'

'If you can't see, or don't want to see, I should be the last one to cause mischief.'

Judith saw one of David's most characteristic lunges of the arm as he turned towards Bronwen, emphasizing a point, either lightly striking her shoulder or just missing it. In this light it was hard to be sure. But even in this light there was an instant when she could have sworn that Caspian had half made a move to knock the arm away.

'I never did understand why you let David invite such extraordinary people here.'

'They are old friends of ours,' said Judith.

'Both of them?'

'Yes, both of them.' It came out more defiantly than she had intended.'

'Hm. Personally I find her most peculiar. A woman in her position, and in trade.'

'You can hardly call it that, mother. She's a very highly esteemed specialist in her own field.'

'In trade,' repeated Lady Brobury. 'Well, if that's what he fancies . . .'

'Caspian? He's devoted to her, of course.'

'Don't be so naïve, my dear. I'm talking about your husband, not hers. It's time you realized: husbands go through humours of their own at a time like this.' Lady Brobury glanced at the swell of Judith's waistband and made a moue of disgust. 'That young woman's very attractive, and well she knows it. So does David. Just like his father.'

It was all irrelevant. David was her husband, father of the child waiting to be born, and they had been so happy and would be happy again. A few weeks from now there would be the baby and so many things new, and the months and years would strengthen a boy to run and romp between them, down those lawns and out over the lands which would one day be his. He would see what she saw now, but all of it – the pastures, the parkland, the quiet woods and smooth-bosomed hills – bright and sharp and fresh in the eyes of innocence.

But the onset of evening was darkening her own vision of the landscape. As well as a child's happiness there were the other things: childish disillusionment, nursery fears. The moss creeping over the edge of the terrace took on the shape of a clawing hand. Something reached for her. If she turned her back it would scuttle closer and cut off her escape. Twilight's last orange glow on the hillside was a dim ember which could swiftly be rekindled to scorch its way down and engulf her.

I shall be torn open, and my baby will die before it has ever lived.

Something waits down there in the shadows.

No. It's to be a girl, and born not here but far away. I've already said that, and I did mean it, didn't I?

She pictured David and herself romping down that slope with a stumbling, chuckling little shape between them. Then saw them desolate, with an aching gap between them, an emptiness which could never again be filled.

The doctor had told her that all women had absurd fears at this time. They would pass.

The swish of her movement as she went indoors might have been a signal: a maid came in with a large oil lamp, followed by a footman with a taper to light the wall lamps. When the windows had been closed and the curtains drawn, Lady Brobury warmed her hands at the fire in the grate and said with implacable maternal authority: 'You surely know something of a man's deplorable appetites by now. What they demand of we poor women!'

'I don't find my husband's affection deplorable.'

'I always found that kind of thing revolting, quite revolting.' Lady Brobury grimaced again. 'And even more despicable that they should be so without restraint, all of them. An unchaste wife would enrage them; yet they revel in unchastity wherever else it can be found.'

'Mother, if you think for a moment that – '

'Just like his father. The moment it was confirmed that I was enceinte I made Mortimer keep his distance. As any respectable woman would. But while I waited obediently to do my duty and provide him with an heir, there he was, off across the fields. Riding off to this village and that one. Not just Mockblane but Lenhale and anywhere else he might gratify himself. Even with serving girls in this very house, while I was abed.'

'You weren't imagining all this?'

'Not then and not now, my girl. Not like some. Where do you suppose David spends all those days now that you're of no use to him?'

'I don't believe it. I won't.'

'Go away to Hereford and leave him, and there'll be the nights as well as the days.'

'Is that why' – Judith was startled by the hoarseness of her own voice – 'you've been so set against my going?'

'What other reason should there be?'

There was the sound of Bronwen and the two men returning, coming in by the side door past the gun-room. Footsteps went upstairs; others approached the drawing-room, and Judith recognized her husband's tread. She braced herself to meet him.

Lady Brobury was already on her way to the door. 'It has lasted too long,' she said. 'High time there was a reckoning, for all our sakes.'

She swept past David as he came in.

He looked hesitant – a gawky, nervous boy uncertain of the best way of breaking some bad news or asking a difficult question. When he kissed her on the forehead it was a tentative peck of a kiss, and he must have felt her flinch away.

At once he was blustering. 'Look here, my love. What exactly does go on in that maze?'

'I think I'll have half an hour's rest before dinner.'

'You haven't answered my question.'

'There isn't any answer. Nothing goes on in the maze that I know of.'

'But you're always in there.'

'I occasionally stroll in there, just as I stroll everywhere else in the grounds.'

'There's something unhealthy about it.'

'Unhealthy? In wanting a brief spell to myself now and then?'

'Spell . . . yes, in every sense, that's it, isn't it? A spell. First mother's drawn under it, and now you. And neither of you can tell me a word about it. Why this craving? Do the two of you go in together?'

'Whyever should we do that?'

'Bronwen tells me there's something in there which is having a bad effect on you.'

'Bronwen does, does she? What has it to do with her?'

'You know how she and Caspian work together – the close rapport they have. I asked them to stay on a few days, to keep you company. To see what they might do to help.'

'You think I need help?'

'I just wanted them to be with you, to . . . well, to sense your worries and see if the maze or anything else offered any clues.'

'To spy on me.'

'No, Judith, that's not true. They're friends, old friends, we both trust them – '

'Do we, indeed?'

'For your own good!' His awkward reasonableness snapped. 'They felt something disturbing when you were in the maze. What they call emanations. I don't understand, and they think you remember nothing of it. *Do* you remember . . . understand any of it?'

'I understand one thing,' she said. 'That's not why you asked them to stay. You thought I'd be away in Hereford, you wanted *her* to be here while I was well out of the way.'

'I didn't ask them until after – '

'I know why,' she said.

Then she went upstairs and sat alone until it was time to make ready for dinner.

At dinner the conversation proceeded in fits and starts, all on uncontentious topics and yet at cross purposes. When Caspian spoke to Judith she was only half listening, straining to catch what David might be saying to Bronwen even though she knew that here, at this table, it would be of no consequence. For David's part, whenever he caught his wife's eye he hurriedly completed what he was saying and tried to draw her into some more general talk; whereupon she immediately retreated, leaving a chasm of silence.

Caspian said: 'Did you see anything of Laura Hinde before you left London?'

'Not as much as we used to,' said Judith without interest. 'I think there was some young man in the offing, and her father approved, so they were all fully occupied.'

She did not pursue the matter: it had occurred to her that the Hindes had been involved in one of those odd thaumaturgic investigations about which the Caspians were so discreet – or secretive; and that his apparently offhanded query might be meant to lead on to a skilled inquisition into her own private world. That, after all, was why David had postponed the Caspians' departure. Or that, at least, was his excuse. And if it were no more than an excuse, she did not know which alternative she hated the more.

What were David and Bronwen talking about now? He was growing more animated, leaning towards her.

Judith had lost all appetite for food. Her child filled her to overflowing, there was no comfort. Laying down her knife and fork, she made a pretence of wanting to join in David's and Bronwen's conversation. At once it faltered. David straightened up and went on eating.

It struck Judith that Caspian, too, was watching them: watching his wife and David. The tilt of his head indicated an alertness for some faint echo – for which she, too, was listening.

Out of the hush they all began to talk at once, and floundered to a halt. Lady Brobury joined in briskly: of all of them, she was the most truly contented.

That night as David removed the gold cufflinks which Judith had given to him on their wedding day, she said: 'You were very attentive to Bronwen at dinner.'

'Isn't that one of the pleasures of having guests at table – a change of atmosphere, and a change of everyday topics?'

'I bore you.'

'That's ridiculous. Because one makes polite conversation – '

'That's the current name for it, is it?'

'For what?'

'Flirtation. Philandering. Deception.'

'Judith!'

'I'm fat and uninteresting. And who made me thus? Whereas she is a well-read and entertaining young woman from the city who is clever enough not to be weighed down by children. It's a pleasure talking to her, a bore talking to me.'

'Ridiculous.' He looked at her, not directly, but sidelong through the looking-glass.

'I look ridiculous, I know that. And I sound ridiculous. You need not keep repeating it.'

His lips started to speak, then stubbornly tightened. She knew she deserved his disapproval, but that did not make it any better.

She said: 'I'm not well enough to entertain. It's too much to ask of me. I would like your friends to leave as soon as possible.'

'Our friends.'

'To leave,' she said, 'as soon as possible.'

'They have already asked if they may do so,' he said grimly.

'You surprise me.'

'Caspian feels that – '

'Ah, Caspian. I can guess what Caspian feels. Like myself, he would like to see this shabby business brought to a conclusion.'

'I don't understand a word of all this.' He pulled his shirt over his head. His strong, tautly bowed back with the birthmark under his left shoulder tempted her to reach out and touch him. She rejected the impulse. She would not be gullible, would not be manipulated by him or her own weakness for him. 'But since this feeling appears to be general, I'll drive them to Lenhale in the morning.'

'No.'

'One minute you say you want them to go, the next – '

'Crampton can drive them. Or one of the grooms.'

'Unnecessary. And discourteous.'

'A last ride together,' Judith heard herself sneer, 'as the late Mr Browning so romantically put it – is that what you must have?'

'There's no reasoning with you. One day we'll talk about this, my love, and laugh at it. And not believe a word of it.'

A flicker of doubt taunted her momentarily: doubt about what she half remembered, what she ought to have made herself remember, from the maze. She brushed it off. She was not allowed to doubt. A shutter clanged down to protect her from such vagaries, and she said:

'You won't object to my having a bedroom to myself from tomorrow night onwards?'

'This is absurd.'

'On the contrary, it's very sensible. I know I'm growing heavy and displeasing. I must be a great nuisance heaving to and fro in the night, disturbing your rest. You'll sleep the better for my absence.'

'I'll do no such thing.'

'So that's how it will be? But if you absolutely must seek diversion elsewhere, at least it won't be with a friend's wife, under our own roof. Tonight, at least, I'll make sure of your presence.'

He was incapable of answer. Only when he was turning down the lamp did he manage: 'It'll be only the one night, I suppose, until Margaret comes for you.'

'Margaret?' she said vaguely. 'Oh, oh yes.' In some way Margaret had ceased to be of any consequence.

It was a groom and not David who brought the trap round in the morning. Whatever awkward explanations David had forced himself to make, they did not seem to have offended Caspian: indeed, when the two men stiffly shook hands there was positive relief in

Caspian's face, a positive readiness to turn quickly away and be carried quickly from Ladygrove Manor.

David, relieved yet hurt, kept pace with the trap to the gates and stood there waving after his guests.

Judith stood beside Lady Brobury and said: 'I shall need to have one of the maids to help Nancy today – I'm moving into a room of my own for a while.'

'It would have been more seemly for you to have done so many months ago. I'm glad you're taking your responsibilities more seriously.'

'Perhaps it's a lot of trouble, really, just for a night or two. If Margaret comes back tomorrow – '

'Oh, Margaret. I wouldn't count on her coming tomorrow or any other day.'

'But she was most insistent.'

'And now is doubtless being insistent with somebody else about something quite different. No, once Margaret was back in the town I expect she forgot all about us out here.' Lady Brobury watched the last sign of the trap as it went below the trees, towards the bridge. 'With those two out of the way as well, everything's going to be so much easier.'

They had never been apart until now. They had been in different places, had gone about their separate professions and pursued their own personal interests, but had never truly been parted one from the other: there had always been that instinctive communion. Now they sat with knees touching in the cramped space of the trap; and there was a great void between them.

If David had been driving there would have to be some show of banal, non-committal conversation. But behind the groom's rigidly impersonal back there was nothing they could say. They dared not reach out in intimate telepathy: each was afraid of a rebuff, both so much at odds that their talent was blunted and unusable.

This was what Caspian had so often feared. A rift between them was a danger not only to that unique talent but perhaps to the very essence of their being. It robbed them of a necessary faculty just as surely as a street accident or some serious error of judgment on the stage of Count Caspar's theatre could rob the victim of a limb or an eye.

And it was Caspian's fault.

Rationally and analytically he knew this. Of course his wife could not have yielded herself willingly to the ravisher. They had experienced trials and terrors just as disorientating before, surrendering themselves through other minds in order to understand and cure those minds, and had come through shaken but unscathed. This case was no different. Yet here, against all his scientific and philosophical principles, he was playing the crudely jealous husband.

In the silence as they jogged their interminable way round the end of the valley to Lenhale he wondered if Bronwen was, like himself, agonizing over those recriminations which had bruised and then broken their rapport. Once there would have been no need to guess: his mind would have nudged hers and she would wordlessly have answered – unless, in mischievous mood, she chose to tease him with half-glimpses and evasions before they came lovingly in tune. Now he could not reach her.

Back in their own environment, away from Ladygrove, things must surely settle gradually back to normal. Anything else was inconceivable.

He hated turning his back on a task unfinished. At the same time he could not have exposed Bronwen again to what he had felt exulting through her body when she was, by proxy, in the arms of David Brobury.

'Because that's what it was,' he had fiercely accused her when they were shut away in their room on the south-east corner: 'unfaithfulness by proxy. No phantom, no revenant, nothing psychic: simply a depravity in your own lower consciousness, willing itself to life.'

'Not *mine*!' she had flung back at him. 'It was Judith – or whoever Judith has taken upon herself in that maze.'

'There's nothing there to be taken on. The whole tale has provided a useful symbol, nothing more, meaning whatever one wishes it to mean. For old Lady Brobury the legend has been a focus for her religious caprices – her need for some private, personal self-esteem. For Judith the fantasy is that of the husband of whom she has been deprived too long. You were sharing her sexual delirium – and wallowing in it.'

'But it wasn't just hers. What about the anchoress, centuries further back? She was real, too.'

'No.'

'She was real,' Bronwen insisted: 'all those period details, the other people and what they said and did – it couldn't just have been invented.'

'Not pure invention, no; but based unconsciously on things Judith could have read and obviously did read in family records, or for that matter in the most ordinary history book. The symbolism of her sensual frustrations is so clear: the young woman's piety and virginity, the growing lust to surrender that virginity, the breaking open of her physical prison, and the rape that was welcomed because all along she had been seeking a passionate reunion with her own husband.'

'Her own husband,' said Bronwen desperately. 'Just so. Not *I* – not *my* imagining.'

'You as well,' he raged. 'How long have you been nursing this secret desire for David, that you could yield so readily? So blissfully, damn it. That was no scientific investigation you were engaged on: it was the fulfilment of some hunger in your own body.'

'Alex, my love . . . my own love . . . what has this dreadful place done to us?'

Bumping to and fro in the trap, he heard again every line of their quarrel and longed to expunge it from memory, from existence altogether. He recognized the logic of Bronwen's own defence. For the first time his logic refused to match hers. Which was illogical, for how could there be two distinct, contrary strands of logic?

He must – and would – discard all unworthy emotions.

Still he felt she had committed adultery.

The distance between their minds grew wider and more dangerous. If at this moment they had been halfway through a case, achieving that precarious entente which was all-important to the unravelling of physical from psychical illness, such discord would have thrown their whole quest into confusion. In the delicate mental surgery needed for psychic injuries or the evil cancer of supernatural forces feeding alongside the natural forces and stresses of the worldly body, it had proved essential for them to work in unswerving telepathic harmony. Conflict in their marriage of minds destroyed all their shared abilities.

Even if David Brobury had again asked them to prolong their stay at Ladygrove Manor there would have been no point now. In their present split state of mind they could have contributed nothing, solved nothing for the Broburys.

Caspian told himself there was nothing to solve for the Broburys. It was all as he had said: a masquerade of personal pretensions and appetites. He would not allow Bronwen to be exposed again to Judith's lecherous daydreams; nor allow her to succumb, knowingly or only half-knowingly, to an infection she might not be able to shake off. He would not have their marriage polluted by the spectre of David Brobury. The most pernicious incubus was that to which a woman involuntarily opened herself.

Yet every mile distancing them from Ladygrove made more hateful the idea of abandoning friends – even if the friendship had now inexcusably soured; abandoning them, he thought as he tried so hard not to think it, to something which became every moment less glibly explicable and more sinister and far-reaching than he had been prepared to acknowledge.

They clattered at last along the narrow street of Lenhale, past the tavern and ostlery, and up the short approach to the railway station. The groom neatly bunched the reins, hitched them to an awning support, and sprang down to offer Bronwen his hand.

'You'll not forget the horse to be collected from the ostler?' said Caspian.

'Jenny, that'll be. No, sir, I got my instructions, thank you.'

He took down the valise and boxes and carried them through to the station platform, stood to one side as Caspian bought tickets from the window, and when he was sure that all was well and the departing guests were adequately equipped for departure he touched the shiny black rim of his hat and turned away towards the ostlery at the foot of the approach.

Caspian drew the gold half-hunter from his waistcoat pocket and compared its time with that of the station clock. They had a full twenty minutes to wait before the train was due.

With the groom gone, they still had nothing to say.

A horse was being meekly backed between the shafts of a cart in the station yard. Out of sight a man was shovelling coal, the swish of his shovel becoming a screech as every now and then it struck stone flooring. A dog began to bark.

Bronwen said: 'Pippin – the Broburys' dog – if it did follow Margaret all the way here, she may have lodged it in the stable as well.'

'They'll mention it, then.'

'We've got plenty of time. I'll walk down and make sure.'

It was an excuse to be away from him, if only for a few minutes. He watched her go: his wife, his incomparable wife, slim and graceful in her carriage yet with a Welsh sturdiness which added determination to her gentlest movement, rapier steel to her most lilting remark. Had he not the right to be jealous over such beauty? Many a man in history had had to fight to possess such beauty, and fight with sword and savagery to retain it. Faithfulness in thought, word and deed. And for her, the same faithfulness. In thought . . .?

She was in the doorway at the end of the approach, beckoning. There was no mental alarm, such as he might normally have heard; but the gesture was in itself urgent enough.

He strode down to join her.

She said: 'The dog isn't here. No mention of it at all.'

'If you're talking about Pippin, ma'am,' said the groom, deferential but puzzled, 'he does wander. But only a few hours, and then home again.'

'He didn't go home,' said Bronwen.

Caspian shrugged. 'The lady said nothing about a dog when she left the mare?' he asked the ostler.

'Ah, but it weren't no lady, sir. This mare, she were brought in by a man.'

Bronwen glanced at Caspian to convey that this was what had disturbed her.

He refused to be disturbed. He had had enough of Ladygrove and its valley and its neighbouring villages and all the tempers and temperaments of the Brobury family. 'Mrs Henderson was probably late for her train, and paid someone to take charge of Jenny and bring her in here. The beast's safely here, anyway, so plainly the fellow was reliable.'

'Oh, I knew him all right, sir.' The ostler was obsequiously anxious to please. 'Brought up in Lenhale, he was, before going into Sir Mortimer's service.'

'Oh, one of the Brobury staff?'

'Ten years and more, sir. Though I'd say he was more used to prodding pigs than handling horses these days.'

'Pigs?' exclaimed Bronwen.

'Oh.' The groom slapped the mare's flank as if in commiseration. 'Evan Morris, eh?'

It was innocent enough, straightforward enough. The swineherd had chanced to be in his home village when Margaret arrived, and had taken charge of Jenny and stabled her according to orders. Caspian could almost hear Margaret rasping out the orders. But he also heard himself asking:

'You didn't see the lady at all, then?'

'No, sir, can't say I did.'

'The train would have come in just about then, I suppose.'

'Well ...' The ostler scratched his head. 'Funny, but I don't recollect hearing it when we was talking. You usually gets a right old earful when it comes in over the crossing, and then when it go out again. But there, I wasn't paying no special attention. Could have come and gone without me so much as noticing, most likely.'

Caspian took Bronwen's arm and drew her outside. The groom led Jenny out and took her to the trap, fastening her by a loose rein so that she could trot behind. Slowly he drove back down the approach, touched his hat again as he passed, and set a careful and steady pace back the way along which he had brought them to the station.

Bronwen said: 'You know there's something wrong, don't you?'

'We've finished with Ladygrove and its petty problems.'

'There's something wrong and,' she insisted, 'you know it.'

'Margaret arrived here just in time for the train, saw one of the estate workers she knew, handed over the mare, and caught the train and went on her way. There's nothing to suggest otherwise.'

Bronwen stood erect and untouchable; yet demanding that he touch her, if only with the fingertips of his mind.

'Nothing?' she challenged.

He looked at a path meandering up the hillside above the village and wondered if that was the short cut to Ladygrove, over the ridge and along the side of the vale and down through the Brobury woods and parkland.

'If we had kept Jenny,' he said, 'one of us could have ridden her back along that route – just to make sure everything was in order.'

'And then on to Ladygrove, to deliver her home and explain? And how would one explain?'

He laughed shortly. Reluctantly they exchanged the sketch of a smile. There was the faint, uncertain tingle of a rapprochement.

'If we go at all,' he said, 'we'll have to walk.'

'If necessary, yes.'

'Or hire two hacks from the ostler.'

'But we're going, aren't we?' she said.

'Yes,' said Caspian, 'I'm afraid we have to.'

❧ 5 ❧

The path was easy enough to follow. It began behind the stumpy little market cross and crawled its way over the hill in a long, laborious zigzag which avoided the steeper inclines and occasionally sagged downhill, skirting an outcropping elbow before resuming its slow ascent.

'You left something behind then, sir, ma'am?' The ostler had shown deferential amusement, preparing to make some small profit out of the mishap. 'You'd best let me keep an eye on your luggage for you, and we'll treat it as a deposit on two horses, like?'

He had hired out to them two leisurely hacks which sometimes plodded side by side, sometimes fell one behind the other along the narrowing track. Caspian at such times took the lead and quickened the pace. When they came to a spacious ride through the first stretch of woods, he fell back beside Bronwen.

They jogged on, staring ahead, each waiting for the other to speak first.

'Are we being silly?' Caspian asked at last. 'What makes us interfere in a mystery which may be no mystery at all?'

Her lips pursed ruefully. 'You think I've rushed us into it – made another misjudgment?'

'If you did, we shared it. We both felt something was wrong. But are we both too sensitive to nuances which for other people add up to nothing of importance?'

Crows squawked in swaying treetops high above. A hare emerged from the grass beside the path, rose on his hind legs and raised a patrician nose to savour the air, then lolloped across in front of them and plunged again to earth.

The trees were thinning out, and ceased altogether on the crown of the ridge. Bronwen and Caspian drew rein and looked down into the valley beyond. Mockblane church was just visible three miles away. On a stretch of golden field, tiny figures moved in a swinging dance, and every now and then the sun flashed from a scythe blade. Ladygrove Manor was hidden behind its sheltering spur, inked over on this side by dark clusters and blobs of woodland.

'Do you hear anything?' asked Bronwen.

The note of discouragement in her voice asked if they were wasting their time. Caspian was glad that David Brobury knew nothing of this impulse which had driven them inquisitively back along Margaret's route. When it all proved a false alarm, they could ride back to Lenhale, return the horses, and pay the ostler to keep his mouth shut.

'We'll try another mile or so down into the valley,' he suggested. 'Not too close to Ladygrove, or the harvesters, in case David's out on his rounds.'

The path was lumpy and required some care for the first quarter of a mile. Then the woods began again, and there was another ride, cut well back to either side, a shimmering green swathe descending between palisades of dark tree trunks.

They were well into the long avenue when they got the first intimation, like the faintest shrill of an alien bird-call, quite out of place in this setting. Caspian slowed his mount, automatically alert for Bronwen to think herself into unison with him.

Her green eyes were hazed with sadness, as dull as the underside of a drooping leaf.

'Let me in.' He could not be sure whether she had said it aloud or whether she was forcing herself imploringly against his mental barrier. He tried to open to her. In this they must be together: must resonate to the same distant cry.

For there had been a cry, he was sure of it.

They halted, a yard apart. Her horse snuffled and then was still.

There was a faint chink of harness, and through it the fainter discord of a despairing, incoherent mind wailing from the depths of the forest.

Further on.

This time there were no words. They agreed, they were drawing closer together.

They eased the animals forward. Very slowly they went on down the wide, long ride. At one moment the sound grew fainter, and they stopped and trotted the horses round in a slow circle until the direction was clear again. They had reached a wooden rail projecting halfway across the avenue and marking for some distance a narrower path striking off at right angles. At the junction of the two ways was a wide patch of trampled earth – a pattern of muddy lumps and holes which had hardened into deep, convoluted ruts. Guiding the horses around the worst hazards, they edged into the wood. Now Caspian had to lead again, and the cry weakened, but was strong again as they came side by side into a clearing. Beyond this it would be impossible to take the horses.

Now there could no longer be any doubt. As they dismounted and walked on they knew it had not been a matter of wayward imagination, they had not been mistaken in setting out. Haltingly, still not entirely at ease with each other but striving to overcome the mistrust, they clutched at thoughts which had no words, an emotion which was more anger than fear.

It was rising to a shout. Ahead was another clearing. Crossing it, their feet sank into a soft beech mast. On its far side, like a broad sawn-off trunk, was something too square and even to be other than man-made. It was a hut about five feet high, and of roughly the same depth and width. A stake had been driven into the ground a few feet from the door, with something clamped on top which might have been a wad of sacking or some discarded twist of ragged leather. When Bronwen and Caspian reached it they saw that it was neither.

From the top of the stake Pippin's head leered at them – jaws open to reveal grinning teeth, blind eyes staring balefully. Dried blood from the torn throat had congealed on the stake.

Bronwen put her knuckles into her mouth and bit on them. She desperately wanted to be sick. But she rallied. The sound of their feet crunching and rustling towards the hut had drawn a sound from it that was no longer in their heads but real and clamorous.

'Who's there? Who is it?'

There was no window, but the door of the hut hung slightly askew to create a narrow gap at the top. Fingertips groped over the rough woodwork and tried to shake it.

'It's all right, Mrs Henderson. We'll have you out of there in a moment.'

No lock secured the door, but a thick branch had been knocked through the hasp to wedge it on to the staple. Caspian had to search through the undergrowth for another stub of wood with which to hammer and prise it free. He tugged the door open. Margaret reeled out. They caught her between them and guided her away from the fetid darkness of the hut.

Margaret's nails were broken where she had tried to batter or wrench her way free. Her hair was lank, her face and dress smeared by a dozen different stains. She let out one strangled sob, then pushed herself away from them to stand resolutely on her own two feet.

'I'm obliged to you, Dr Caspian. Mrs Caspian. And now there'll be a reckoning.' Her voice was hoarse but determined. 'I swear when I get my hands on that ruffian, that lunatic . . .'

She saw the dog's head on the stake. Tottering round it, she stared into the dead, distorted face. Their arms were ready for her as she slumped into a faint.

'I never heard anything so ridiculous in my life.' It was at least the fifth or sixth time that Lady Brobury had loftily, indignantly said it.

They were sitting by the fireside: she, Judith, Bronwen and Caspian. The room was warm but the atmosphere far from cosy. Sitting upright on her chair as on a throne, Lady Brobury made no attempt to hide her displeasure at the reappearance of the Caspians or at the story which, she as good as implied, they had extravagantly invented.

'Morris quite properly and sensibly found the mare straying near Lenhale and lodged it at the ostler's until he could report to us. What could he possibly have had to do with Margaret's silly escapade?'

'Being imprisoned in a swineherd's hut and left to die is hardly an escapade, Lady Brobury,' said Caspian respectfully; 'and hardly due to her own silliness, one would think.'

'Imprisoned? The girl must have been having the vapours. Just because she was foolish enough to shut herself in – '

'*I* was not having the vapours,' Bronwen contributed, 'and I clearly saw that the door had been deliberately jammed from outside with a branch.'

'Ridiculous,' said Lady Brobury yet again. 'We shall soon see what Morris has to say to these outrageous accusations.'

Margaret was upstairs sleeping off the exhaustion of her ordeal. David had gone off in a fury to get his hands on the swineherd, announcing that he would bring him back here at whatever hour of the night it might be. Until then, and until Margaret was recovered enough to give a coherent account of her misadventures, they had little to go on. Little as it was, Lady Brobury had already made up her mind: indifferent to her daughter's well-being, she was regally determined to protect her cherished swineherd from whatever calumnies might be devised.

Caspian tried to suppress a mounting antagonism. Simply by existing, the tetchy old woman was an eternal source of dissension within her family. Along with the antagonism went a mounting suspicion. He refused any longer to see her as the helpless, hard-done-by widow she tiresomely presented herself as being. But still he could not be sure how exactly he did see her.

Abruptly he said: 'And the dog? Was that the vapours, too – its own foolishness – getting itself decapitated?'

Judith gasped. 'No! You don't mean Pippin?'

'Alex,' Bronwen begged. 'Surely you don't have to – '

'Somebody' – Caspian stared at Lady Brobury and saw that she had no intention of flinching – 'cut off Pippin's head and stuck it on a post.'

Judith whimpered, gagged; Bronwen leaned closer and put a hand firmly on her arm.

'How can you be so callous?' said Lady Brobury. 'Judith my dear, this is all becoming so distasteful. I'm sure you would feel better in bed.'

Judith did in fact make a move to get up. Before she could heave her weight from the chair, however, there was the crash of the front door closing. David marched in, driving Evan Morris before him as if the man had been one of his own hogs.

'Margaret still resting?'

'As we all should be. You certainly can't disturb her at this time.'
Lady Brobury was, of a sudden, solicitous.

'I heard you come up the stable-yard.'

Margaret stood in the doorway behind her brother. She had pulled
a woollen dressing-gown over her nightgown, and her hair was
drawn back into a hastily woven bun.

'You can't show yourself like that,' protested Lady Brobury. 'It's
most unseemly. If there's anything to discuss it can very well be
settled without having to drag you from – '

'I want it settled,' said Margaret, 'in my presence. Without delay.'
She advanced into the room and stopped by Evan Morris's shoulder.
He kept his head very still. She sniffed once, twice; and said with
loathing: 'It was you. I'll swear it was you.'

'Your ladyship, I don't know what all this is about. I swear I don't.'

'Be quiet,' snapped David. 'You'll speak when you're spoken to.
And now, let's go over it from the beginning.'

His mother clapped a hand to her head. 'It's cruel. All this noise,
this bullying. I don't know how I'm expected to sleep tonight. My
head . . .'

'It might be better if you did go to bed, mother. I'll get Jenkins to
see you to the lodge.'

'I think it would be better if Lady Brobury stayed,' said Caspian.

She bestowed an icy glare on him. 'I have every intention of
staying, Dr Caspian, without needing to seek your permission.'

David took his sister's elbow and led her to an armchair by the
fire. She was beginning to tremble, and held out her hands to the
warmth. David turned to Caspian, but still kept an eye on the sullen,
hunched figure of the swineherd.

'Now. Alex, will you be good enough to tell us what you found
this morning?'

Stirred by renewed jealousy and the memory of Bronwen's sensual
dream torment, Caspian quelled his instinctive hostility. David's
decisiveness in tracking down Evan Morris and bringing him here
so promptly deserved as brisk a response. Friendly and serious,
Caspian said:

'Ought we not to start at the beginning, with Margaret's experiences?'

'Of course. You're quite right. Margaret – '

'By whose authority,' demanded Lady Brobury, 'is Dr Caspian imposing himself on this fruitless inquiry?'

'Margaret,' said David, 'will you tell us what happened when you left here on Jenny yesterday morning?'

She clasped her hands together, slowly rubbing them. It was clear that she would not speak until she was sure her voice would be steady.

She began: 'You all saw me go, so you know what time it was. I was riding Jenny, and the dog . . .' She faltered, then made herself continue. 'Pippin followed me. I kept shouting at him to go home, and whisking my riding crop at him, but he just trotted along behind.'

'Quite uncontrollable,' murmured her mother. 'Quite useless.'

Margaret had set a steady pace which would get her to Lenhale in time for any mid-morning train there might be. If she found when she arrived that there was time to spare, she was quite prepared to order an early lunch at the inn, after stabling Jenny. It was a mild, pleasant morning, and she enjoyed the ride. Years before she had come along this route more than once with her father. There were few striking landmarks, but she tried to pick out plantations which had been young when she was young, and to guess in advance what side path or firebreak lay beyond the next gentle rise, around that next clump of oaks.

The noises of the woodland were so different from the Malayan forests through which she had travelled sometimes with her husband. A few evoked moments of her childhood; others had been forgotten, or were new to her. Breeze and birdsong, rustling of leaves and the thud of Jenny's hoofs, all fitted into a pattern.

But then there was a snuffling and whistling which at first she could not identify. It came from the fringes of the wood on her right, just as the avenue along which she rode was beginning to narrow.

'Swine rooting for acorns?' suggested Caspian quietly.

Evan Morris shook his head resentfully.

Lady Brobury said: 'Don't put words into the girl's mouth.'

'I didn't know what it was,' said Margaret, 'but it seemed to follow me, crashing along just inside the wood, keeping pace with the horse.' She stared into the leaping flames.

She had ridden a few hundred yards further when the noise began to worry Pippin. Instead of bounding along behind, pausing for an occasional sniff in the bracken and a game with some fallen twig, he came closer to Jenny's hoofs, whining, looking up as if for protection. Then he began to growl and make little sorties towards the edge of the wood, but without actually plunging in between the trees.

All at once the noises ceased. There was a strange lull. Margaret urged the mare onward, eager to reach the top of the slope and go over the ridge above Lenhale. But the dog did not follow. It stopped, pointed, and then suddenly with a violent barking launched itself into the darkness.

Then it screamed. The horse reared. Pippin streaked out of the trees again, almost under Jenny's forelegs. She whinnied, shied away, and stumbled. Margaret felt herself sliding sideways. She tried to hold on, but Jenny was down and she went down with her. Rolling clear, she was aware of Pippin madly circling them both and dashing back through the trees. Hysterical barking became a scream again. The mare answered, scrambling to her feet, shuddering, and galloping off along the ride. Margaret shouted. The mare went faster. The only response was one final, awful yelp from Pippin; then silence.

Silence save for a heavy crashing through the bushes, and a sudden snort of what might have been laughter or hatred. Before Margaret could get to her feet and look round, a hand was clamped over her mouth. A fist drove brutally into her back and began to force her off the path and in through the trees. She struggled, tried to kick back, but was driven onwards. Ahead was a clearing; and on the far side of the clearing was a hut. She hoped for a wild second, as her captor reached past her to drag the door open, that she could wriggle free and turn on him. But he clamped her even closer, thrusting his head against her neck, and once the door was half-open hurled her forward so that she smacked into the far wall. Robbed of breath, she collapsed on the stinking floor. Before she could get even to her knees, the door grated shut and the light was blocked out.

She shouted, but there was no answer. She went on shouting. And then, when she knew that no one would hear, she began pulling and kicking and clawing at the door.

'And the man who threw you in,' prompted Caspian when David,

125

staring lividly at Evan Morris, seemed incapable of framing a question: 'did you see his face?'

'No.'

'No way of identifying him?'

'He stank,' said Margaret, 'of pigs.'

'Sheer imagination,' said Lady Brobury. 'Ideas they've put in your head. Obviously you fell foul of a poacher, who didn't dare let you see his face and bundled you into the hut. There's no more to it than that.'

Evan Morris turned ponderously towards her. An insolent grin creased the grime of his face and faded slowly, complacently.

David said: 'And the poacher fastened the door so that she could die of starvation?'

'He probably only wanted time to get away. He'd have guessed someone would come along and find her.'

'Alex, you and Bronwen were the ones who did find Margaret. What made you turn back and look for her?'

'Yes,' said Lady Brobury thinly, 'what *did* make you start prying, Dr Caspian?'

'I'll not have it called prying.' Margaret's face flushed with more than the heat of the fire. 'If they hadn't come in search of me I'd have been left for dead.'

'Alex?'

Caspian positioned himself by the end of the mantelpiece. He looked down on their faces in the flickering light: all upturned save for the swineherd's. Morris stood back from the group with his head averted, apparently studying a far corner of the carpet.

Caspian described his arrival with Bronwen at Lenhale and the casual enquiry at the ostlery which ceased to be casual. He glossed over the true nature of their unease: in such company it was simpler and safer to talk of sudden impulses than of psychic powers slowly reawakening. 'We felt there was something wrong,' he hurried on. 'It . . . well, let's just say it gave us the fidgets. We hired two horses and rode part of the way back.'

'But how did you know where I would be?' Margaret was looking curiously up at him.

'How *did* you?' Her mother intervened again. 'If there's anyone who arouses my suspicion, it's you, Dr Caspian. How could you have known about the hut, and about Margaret being in it?'

They would not understand and must not be allowed to understand. 'We didn't know,' said Caspian with a barely perceptible hesitation. 'We spent some time moving about before we heard her.'

'Heard her?'

'Yes,' said Caspian firmly: 'heard her.'

Margaret was shaking her head uncertainly. Before she could raise troublesome doubts, Caspian took over the inquisition without David realizing that the initiative had passed from his hands.

'You claim,' he said over the heads of the others to the swineherd, 'that you found Jenny, the mare, wandering near Lenhale village.'

'That I did.'

'Why didn't you bring her back here where she belonged?'

'Not much of a hand with horses, I'm not. And that Jenny's always been a bit on the skittish side. I'd be afear'd to go far with that 'un. Only Sir Mortimer rightly knew how to handle 'un.' Morris managed to make it a sly reproach, aimed at the back of Margaret's head. 'Safest thing was to get her to Harwood the ostler, and leave her there to be picked up.'

'Why didn't you report the fact to Sir David here, or to Lady Brobury?'

'Didn't have no cause to come right back over the estate, not right away. As soon as I was here I'd ha' done it – first thing tomorrow, most likely.'

'Or never?'

'You got no cause to say things like that to me, mister.'

'If nobody was aware that Mrs Henderson had not even reached Lenhale on Jenny – '

'I didn't know nothing about Mrs Henderson. Didn't know what that horse was doing there, and never had no call to ask. Did what I thought best, that was all.'

'That hut in the woods is yours?'

'There's a couple I use, yes, when the weather turns nasty. Not much call to be there this time o' year.'

'So that once Mrs Henderson had been shut in there, and nobody knew that she had failed to reach Lenhale and caught the Hereford train, she could have remained there for . . . how long?' Caspian's gaze swung to his right so that Lady Brobury lay in the path of his challenge. 'How long would it have been before anyone commented on Mrs Henderson's disappearance? You here at Ladygrove would have thought she must be busy in Hereford. Her housekeeper there would have assumed her to be still at Ladygrove. How long before people got round to comparing notes: four days, five days – a week? And why' – he spun back towards Morris – 'was she imprisoned in the first place?'

'No use asking me . . . sir.'

Silently Bronwen said: *Because Margaret must not be allowed to reach Hereford.*

'Because,' said Lady Brobury, 'that dog flushed out a poacher. Is it not perfectly plain? The dog got the man's scent and went wild, the fellow killed it, and then pushed Margaret out of the way before she could see his face. That's why.'

In shaky unison Bronwen and Caspian shared it: *Because Judith must not be allowed to leave Ladygrove, must not be taken away by Margaret, that's why.*

Caspian was horrified by the strain of keeping in tune with Bronwen. That corrosive jealousy had done incalculable damage to their loving, unquestioning complicity.

'Where were you' – he forced himself to concentrate on the swineherd – 'at the time Mrs Henderson was riding from here to Lenhale?'

'How'd I be knowing what time that'd be?'

'Let's say between a quarter past eight and nine o'clock yesterday morning.'

'That's hard to say, now. I don't keep much track of time. But let me see . . . part of the morning I know I was on . . . ah, yes, now. Yes, I'm thinking so.'

Morris stared at Lady Brobury.

She said: 'Morris was here with me at that time.'

'With you?' David voiced the disbelief Caspian was already feeling.

'Gracious, how silly.' Lady Brobury wagged her head contemptuously. 'I wasn't connecting the two things. Of course, that settles the whole ridiculous business. Morris was with me from half-past eight at the latest, no question of that. We were discussing winter feed and pannage and what we might hope for in next year's litters. No question about it.'

'He was with you,' said David, 'and didn't mention the horse he had delivered to the Lenhale ostlery?'

'That was afore I went back over Lenhale way,' said Morris in malevolent triumph. 'Earlier in the morning, that'd be.'

'Half-past eight and quite some while afterwards,' said Lady Brobury. 'So that settles it.'

Caspian cursed to himself. One lame question, one error by David, had steered the whole inquisition down the wrong trail. The defence was so glib; and so false. But who could contest the alibi provided by Lady Brobury? Who would dare, without also daring to accuse her to her face of complicity in the whole perverse affair?

He watched the flicker of firelight on bewildered faces. A coal fell, broke, and flared up, and he saw Margaret turn away, incapable of grappling with what had happened to her; David at a loss; Judith dejected and withdrawn into tired remoteness; and Bronwen as angry and frustrated as himself, smelling wickedness as he smelt it and not knowing how to pursue it to its lair. It was escaping them, mocking them. Biding its time.

And Evan Morris, the swineherd: what hold did he have on Lady Brobury, that he should be able to twist what words and excuses he needed from her so readily?

'If there's nothing else then, Sir David.' Morris was standing with shoulders squared, sneeringly sure of himself.

David's arms flagged his despair. 'Very well. But we'll talk again tomorrow. You haven't heard the last of this.' It was an empty threat. But as Morris slouched towards the door and paused only to exchange a last glance with Lady Brobury, David asked wildly into nowhere: 'Where exactly did all this take place – where did you come off the mare, Margaret?'

Margaret and Caspian, both seeing the spot so clearly again, started to speak at once: saw at once the junction of main avenue and side track, the rail barring half the ride, the bare patch of badly rutted earth.

It was Margaret who finished the sentence.

'You see!' Lady Brobury sat back. 'Jenny put her foot in a rabbit-hole.'

'But that's the very place where father met his accident!' cried David. 'And the horse shied and went down . . . again?'

Morris and Lady Brobury were still looking at each other. In the second before their glances snapped away, Bronwen and Caspian shared a topsy-turvy, fragmented vision of what the swineherd and his patroness had shared. If only they had been more closely linked, if only they had been single-minded and less wary of each other still, they might have seen it whole and clear. But there, splintered yet briefly identifiable, it was.

Sir Mortimer was galloping up that same ride. The same rail was there, the same patch of denuded earth. And there was something dashing at his horse's forelegs: Jenny's legs and stumbling hoofs, but not Pippin beneath them. It could have been a tiny, terrified pig. Or a vicious one.

He was down. There was pain in his right shoulder, and his right leg had twisted under him. As he struggled to shift into a more tolerable position, the horse reared up beside him and was off in wild flight; and there were fat shapes close to the ground, busy bustling shapes leaping greedily out of the woodland shadows. They came tearing at him with snouts ready to nuzzle him down, tusks to slash and rend.

Then they were gone. Avenue and woods were gone, the room was restored. Firelight spurted and subsided.

The door closed behind Evan Morris.

But the past had not been closed off swiftly enough. Through the distorted vision of Lady Brobury and her swineherd, Caspian and Bronwen had witnessed the death of Sir Mortimer Brobury. And they knew, sharing the foresight and hindsight of those other two, that it had been no accident.

6

Judith said: 'But I don't want to leave. It was silly of me to make such a fuss about it. This is my home, and it'll be the baby's home.'

Margaret expelled breath in a snort rather than a sigh. She had led Judith round to the coach-house and rapped the newly repaired wheel with her knuckles as if she personally had been responsible for its restoration; and now she was impatient to see it turning.

'David went to a lot of trouble to have this done. And I really can't stay one more day. I've the children to think of, and a hundred things to do. And *you've* a child to think of. You're close to your time.'

'Yes,' said Judith. 'And this is where my child is meant to be born.'

'But we agreed – '

'I didn't know how silly I was being. Now I'm over it.'

'We'll see what David has to say about that. After all we've done. After all I've gone through!'

Margaret stalked irascibly into the house.

Judith looked at her reflection in the polished paintwork of the carriage door. The slight curve of the door made her appear even more swollen than she actually was. The image slid away as she walked on across the stable-yard, floating off the woodwork into nothingness, just as that phantom woman had blurred and disappeared forever after the exorcism.

She looked back from the corner of the yard. Only a week or two ago, she had been so anxious to climb into the coach and be carried away. Today she had said aloud that she no longer wanted to leave Ladygrove.

Strange. So strange. She felt that there were two of her, but one had only emerged and begun to take control since . . . Since when?

She wondered where the other, worried Judith had gone. For herself she was no longer troubled. She would let herself be carried wherever it was right – but not carried away from these grounds.

Lady Brobury was standing at the gate of her lodge. Judith made a long sweep of the garden to pass her on the way down to the maze. Her mother-in-law waited patiently for her to reach the gate.

'They want me to go,' said Judith. 'But I can't go away now, can I?'

'It would be very wrong.'

'It's the others who ought to go away.'

'Quite right, my dear. The fuss these interfering people have caused!'

'I won't go.'

'Be guided by your own heart. It will tell you what to do.'

Lady Brobury remained at the gate and went on placidly watching Judith as she went down towards the peace of the maze.

Peace – but not the peace of somnolence. It was a living, breathing organism, and Judith was becoming part of it. Sometimes with one part of her mind she seemed to see the labyrinth from outside, from above, as if she were floating over its convolutions: it was a diagram, then, of a bloodstream, its coils weaving in and out, but always commanded by the centre, that pulsing heart whose beat grew daily stronger – just as her son's heart within her pounded more strongly and eagerly.

Judith reached the footbridge.

David, half running down the grass, was there at the same moment.

'Judith, you're not to go in there.'

'I need some time to myself.'

'You can have it when we get to London.'

'London?' she said vaguely. The name had a pleasurable ring, and there were other friendly, reminiscent echoes behind it.

'I'm taking you there now,' he said. 'We're going together, just as you've wanted us to.'

She shook her head. Yes, it had been an enjoyable idea once. It had been terribly important once. Now it did not matter. She heard his voice, but she was looking along the narrow line of the bridge into the woods and the clearing where she could stroll and sit and be at ease. That once-cold slab in the cell had grown so warm and comforting.

'Judith, you're not listening.'

She turned to him, and as he tried to take her in his arms his face was close, too close, bending towards her. Suddenly she hated that face: it came out of nightmare at her, the face of a betrayer, one who had ravaged and ravished her but never loved her. And it was his child within her, hated seed of a hated father.

'My dearest, why are you looking at me like that?'

She broke away from him. But now he was blocking the way to the bridge.

She wanted to run, but was too tired.

Now came the others. Bronwen and Caspian were on their way towards her, closing in on her: friends who were no longer friendly, persistent in their attempts to lead her footsteps astray, away from the truth.

'It'll be a bit of a squash for a few miles,' said Caspian cheerfully, as if everything could now be taken for granted. 'We'll manage, though. See you safely on your way.'

'But I'm not going anywhere,' said Judith.

She faced David and waited for him to step aside. He made no move. She tried to advance on him, but faltered. He was too strong and would be too brutal.

Slowly she began to walk back towards the house.

Behind her she heard the murmur of the two men conferring. Plotting against her, as she had heard them plotting last night. Caspian's voice at the foot of the stairs: 'David, it's essential that you get Judith away from here – you personally, to make sure of it, without delay.'

Margaret was waiting for her. They would give her no quarter.

'There we are, then.' Margaret was bright and assertive. 'All packed and ready to leave.'

Judith shook her head again. There was no point in arguing with any of them.

She was hemmed in from behind. At her shoulder David said: 'All of us. All ready.'

Judith took them by surprise by turning and holding out her hand. 'Goodbye, Bron. Goodbye, Alex. You must come and see us again when the baby's born. When . . . when everything has been put right. We'll have so much more time to spare then.'

133

'We are *all* going,' said David steadily. She would not even glance into that wicked face. 'You, Margaret, Bronwen, Alex. And myself. All of us.'

'No.'

'Yes. There are going to be no mistakes this time.'

She was being abducted; kidnapped. There were too many of them. They were hemming her in ever more tightly, like some dangerous prisoner who might make a bolt for it.

Still she might be rescued. Lady Brobury was approaching.

'Cruel,' she said. 'Cruel, David. First you neglect her on the excuse that you've too much work to do. Now you dismiss the work and want to rush her away. And I suppose when you get to London there'll be too much to do, there. So much to occupy you. Just like your father.'

'I've done your packing as well as my own.' Margaret overrode her mother, and tried to jolly her sister-in-law along towards the house.

'But how do you know what I'd want to take?'

'I know what you'll need. Don't worry. I won't let you go short of anything.'

In a way it was a relief to succumb. If they would not let her be, then she must give in. The responsibility was theirs. If someone, somewhere else, would not look after her, then she had no choice but to go along with them.

Nevertheless it was hard to believe that she was really leaving Ladygrove.

Surely it was folly, when she must so soon return?

Margaret went indoors with her. Margaret had become a bluff busybody of a nursemaid. There was no resisting her. Judith's own maid cowered well back. And when Judith asked, 'But will there be room for Eileen?' she received only an airy, 'Oh, David says he will make other arrangements in London.' When they came out again to find the carriage waiting, and Judith, cowed, stepped in, she felt that Margaret only just restrained herself from patting her on the head, as one would pat an obedient dog.

The dog . . . Judith thought of Pippin, and shuddered. But then, it must have deserved its fate. It had been opposing . . . opposing what? Something right and inevitable which must come to fulfilment.

She was being carried away from all that.

Lady Brobury came close to the carriage door. 'It's all right, my dear. They're being intolerably stupid, but you mustn't worry. You'll come back.'

'Of course we'll come back, mother,' said David impatiently, 'when it's right for Judith to come back.'

'It's too late for them to do any lasting harm,' said his mother.

As the carriage gathered speed between the gateposts and down the hill, Margaret said: 'That's so typical of mother, you know. Always making meaning remarks without any real meaning. And then putting on that weightily mysterious air of hers. I really don't know what you're going to do with her, David.'

David's hand closed over his wife's. Caspian, tactfully averting his gaze, nevertheless saw from the corner of his eye how Judith flinched away.

The two of them sat side by side, with the Caspians and Margaret squeezed on to the facing seat. It would be less crowded after Lenhale: Bronwen and Caspian would collect the luggage they had left there and take a train to Hereford to meet a London connection, while the Broburys went on to Hereford at their own more leisurely pace.

Looking out of the window, Caspian conjured up in the opening a memory of Lady Brobury's face as she made her farewells to Judith. The memory was an uneasy one. There were questions he wanted to ask and warnings he was trying to formulate. They could not be discussed in the presence of the others, least of all Judith, and the strain of attempting a telepathic conversation with Bronwen would be too great. Later they would talk.

And would that be too late?

On one thing at least he relied: Judith's removal from Ladygrove Manor ought to put her out of danger. Even without knowing precisely what the danger was, he was convinced of this.

Still the sense of Lady Brobury's insidious presence fretted him. Was she in fact only the warped old woman delineated by Margaret, striving clumsily to improve her standing in the eyes of others by

135

pretending to knowledge which she did not possess, dabbling in amateurish mysticism and hinting at secrets of her own concoction? Or were the private rituals, the exorcism, and the concentration on Judith part of something more sinister?

Something macabre enough to bring about the murder of her husband . . .

The chill in Caspian's mind was more than the chill of advancing autumn. Either the woman was dangerously rather than pathetically mad; or she was being used by some power stronger than herself – used by the swineherd and whatever it was that drove him. Her original vagueness, when they had first come to Ladygrove and first met her, had had all the characteristics of the most successful mediums. Caspian had once scorned the claims of such people; but through intensive investigation he had found among the army of charlatans a few who were genuinely receptive – uncontrolled telepaths, resonating to snatches of thought from the ether, sometimes running graver risks than they realized as their wayward minds grappled with manifestations beyond nature, beyond time and space. Lady Brobury could be one of them, releasing psychic energies of which she was not consciously aware and over which she had no authority.

But her husband: how could there be such a thing as an unwitting murder? One came grimly back to that calculated killing – calculated to ensure that David Brobury would bring his wife to their home and inheritance in time for the birth of their first child.

Questions clamoured in Caspian's head. But now there was another, more turbulent clamour from outside. As the carriage bumped along the village street it was assaulted by shouts and caterwauling from the roadside and from twisting lanes and alleys. Someone was drunkenly singing. Someone else bawled abuse too slurred to be intelligible.

The carriage slowed. David pushed down the window and leaned out.

'Damnation! Some idiot has been ladling out the harvest cider with too generous a hand.'

'Hullo there, squire.'

'Tell him . . . aye, now he's here, tell him we'll not be standing for any more of it . . .'

136

A labourer waving a scythe which threatened to slice off his own ear made a jump on to the coach springs, pressed a mud-streaked face to the edge of the door, and then fell backwards.

'Drive out the harlot . . .'

There was a ragged chorus of curses. Further along the street a scuffle broke out.

'Take your hands off!' David opened the door and sprang down. 'Let go, I say – I order you to let Mr Goswell through. Dimmock, I warn you, you'll be out of your cottage and off my land by nightfall if you don't stand back.'

Caspian got down beside him. They waited as the dishevelled vicar staggered through the throng of villagers. Only the men were in the street: a few wives peered out fearfully between their net curtains, and one or two vainly entreated their menfolk to come inside.

'It's blasphemy,' panted Goswell. 'Sir David, they've run wild. They're desecrating the church.'

'You're the one as has been doing that,' growled one of the nearest men, leaning unsteadily on his pitchfork.

'Papist!'

'Sir David, they must be stopped. The devil's in them, there's no telling what mischief they'll do before the morning's out.'

David closed the door of the carriage on the ladies. The three men turned towards the church. A little knot of labourers came together in the lych-gate, but when David's pace did not slacken they wavered and fell apart. Some scuttled to the far wall of the churchyard and lined up, scared of what they had been doing but drunk enough to want to do more.

'Idolater!'

There was a splintering of glass, and the coloured panes of one of the aisle windows fell out on to the path and a neighbouring headstone.

Mr Goswell agitatedly waved his two companions on into the church.

Half a dozen men with sickles, sheep knives and shepherds' crooks were clawing and scratching at the walls of the chancel. An embroidered banner, slashed across its haloed face, came down. Candles and candlesticks had been thrown from the altar and trampled on the floor.

One man, soberer than the others, was trying to slow them down. 'That'll be enough, now. Take the stuff away, be done with it, but mind the damage. Enough, don't you know when you've done enough?'

David raged up to him. 'What's the meaning of this shameful business, Hopton?'

'There's no holding 'em, Sir David. I've done my best, I swear it. But feelings have been running high, you know. The way our church has been dressed up – it hasn't been right, there's a lot of us against it.'

'But this is no way to settle such matters.'

'No, sir. No.'

'It's as good a way as any,' bellowed one man, stumbling down the chancel steps and steadying himself against the rail.

'It's the drink turned 'em loose, sir,' said Hopton apologetically.

'And their own wickedness,' cried Mr Goswell.

'Wickedness?' A billhook swung erratically. 'And what would you call the goings-on up at the manor, then, if not wicked. Eh?'

'What goings-on?' David demanded.

'Arsk him, if you wasn't there.' The hook was waved under Goswell's nose. 'All that wavin' and mumblin', and unnatural practices.'

'Mr Goswell, does this mean anything to you?'

'Blasphemy and wickedness, that's what it means.'

'We want our church clean and Christian, the way it used to be –'

'Quiet, man! I'll have the lot of you before the magistrates.'

'*He's* the one should be before magistrates. Bringing the Scarlet Woman of Rome into our church.'

The Reverend Frederick Goswell drew himself upright as if preparing for martyrdom.

Caspian thought of the exorcism, and what just one eye-witness's surreptitious inspection and later embroidering of the story could have provoked in the village.

'And what's he keep in there?' The voice was muffled, behind one of the pillars to the side of the chancel.

There was a snarl from the same corner. 'Statues, most likely. Holy pictures. Waiting to put them up – more idolatry!'

David and Caspian hurried under the tower and up the two steps. In the wall opposite the memorial plaque to Matilda was a small wooden door. Two men had their shoulders to it, pushing and grunting. There was a creak of woodwork. At this damp, hitherto neglected end of the church both wood and stonework were rotted and in need of repair.

'Not in there!' David shouted. 'That's the entrance to – '

A crack, and the badly hung door gave way. The two men, caught off balance, reeled in and there was a curse and then a splintering of stone.

David, beside himself with fury, stormed in after them.

'Appalling,' moaned Mr Goswell. 'We are in the Dark Ages again. The Dark Ages!'

Caspian stood in the doorway.

He saw the reason for David's rage. The little door was in fact an inner entrance to the Brobury vault. Light through the outer grille fell across a tier of stone coffins against the west wall, and across four stone plinths in the centre of the mausoleum. Three of the plinths were unoccupied. The fourth was half obscured by a stone coffin which, blundered into by the two hulking rustics, had slid aside and tilted over. One end had cracked, so that the lid was loosened and knocked awry.

The vandals scrambled to their feet, subdued and sobered by the enormity of what they had done.

David stood looking down into the coffin, his face white in the sepulchral twilight. Caspian stepped closer and put a hand on his shoulder. It was the first instinctively friendly contact he had made since seeing David's lascivious face swimming through Bronwen's mind. Now there was only pain and regret in that face.

And what was left of Sir Mortimer Brobury's face stared up at them.

Decomposition had not advanced as far as might have been expected. Where it had eaten away the cheeks and corners of the mouth, the dark and viscous incursions might have been hastened by the tearing of tree stumps and brambles which had already disfigured the features. But looking down into that crumbling corpse, Caspian saw not the ravages of wood and thorns but those of savage tusks and of demented animals biting, tearing, gorging themselves...

In a tremulous voice David said: 'You two men will lift the coffin back on to its table.'

'We didn't mean – '

'Save your breath and do as I tell you.'

Panting, the two of them got below the end of the stone box and managed to slide it upwards against the plinth edge until it could fall back into place. David himself slid the heavy lid across.

'I shall want to see you when you're sober.' His voice was steadier now, and terrifying.

The two men shuffled sideways towards the door, afraid to turn their backs on him.

Caspian took one last look at the coffin. A raised stone plaque on the lid had been engraved with deep, florid letters:

R.I.P.
Mortimer Maxwell Brobury, Bart
beloved husband
of
Charlotte Emilia

The rioters had left the body of the church. Mr Goswell stood in the porch, lean and dark and looking as if he might be capable of putting the evil eye upon each and every member of his congregation. Men were straggling away across the churchyard. One youth was bowed over a grave, vomiting. As David and Caspian brushed past the vicar and trod slowly down the path, there was a sheepish murmuring. Someone growled a curse to make it clear that he had not yet finished what he came to do; but another man edged forward and tried to begin a halting apology.

David cut him short with a savage stab of his hand.

'I'll hear it all,' he said, 'when you've sobered up.'

Margaret's face was framed in the carriage window. Caspian would not have been at all surprised if she had chosen to spring out and join them, or set about the nearer vandals with one of their own sickles.

David said: 'I can't possibly leave now. Not until I've cleared up this disgraceful business and given my bailiff the appropriate instructions. I'll have the ring-leaders out of Mockblane, and make the rest wish they'd never been born.' He glanced back at the porch. 'And I suppose I'll have to do something about Goswell.'

'He's under your mother's thumb.'

'Or she under his. I must say I can't abide the fellow or his methods, any more than my tenants can. But I'll have to stand by him until I've put the rest of them in their place.'

They reached the carriage.

'You have no need to tell us,' said his sister. 'You're staying – yes?'

'I have no alternative.'

'Obviously not.'

Judith leaned across Margaret. 'We shall have to turn back.'

'No. You're to go on.'

'I'm not going,' said Judith, 'without you. I'm coming home. You can't be on your own, with all this going on.'

'I'd be more worried,' said David, 'if you were near.'

'But – '

'Dr and Mrs Caspian will have missed the Lenhale train. I suggest you take them on with you to Hereford. Whether they then find a suitable train to London, or whether they choose to spend a night – '

'I'm afraid I've no spare accommodation to offer,' said Margaret bluntly. 'Judith I can manage, as we planned, but the house really isn't big enough for – '

'Whatever we decide, we'd certainly make our own arrangements,' Caspian assured her.

'If you do stay in the neighbourhood' – was David hinting that he would still like them to keep an eye on Judith? – 'I'll see you when I come through Hereford to collect Judith. If not, we'll meet when we're all back in London.'

Judith was silent, neither protesting nor accepting.

'So,' said Margaret breezily, 'we're back to our first idea – Judith with me, and you collecting her when you've finished what you're doing . . . if you haven't by then found a lot more things requiring your attention.'

'I'll be with you just as soon as I can.'

Caspian got back into the carriage and settled himself beside Bronwen. Margaret had moved across to join Judith. David leaned in to kiss his wife. She offered him her cheek but was trying not to look at him.

'Have a lazy day or two,' he said. 'I won't keep you waiting long.'

The carriage resumed its journey. The street was as unnaturally silent as it had been unnaturally rowdy only half an hour ago.

Caspian thought back to the cracked coffin, the torn face, and the lettering on the lid. To Margaret he said: 'Your mother's Christian name is Charlotte?'

'Charlotte Emilia, yes. Actually it's Charlotte Emilia Gertrude, but she got it into her head that Gertrude sounded terribly common. Mother does have those moods. What makes you ask?'

'I was under the impression I'd heard someone call her Ceridwen.'

'What an extraordinary idea. Who could possibly have called her anything like that?'

'The swineherd, or so I thought. I thought he was referring to your mother, and being rather over-familiar. I assumed it was a Welsh name. There must be plenty of families of Welsh origin along the Marches.'

Bronwen had her head set back against the side of the carriage, staring at him.

'Ceridwen?'

'I'm sure that's what he said. It *is* Welsh, isn't it?'

'Oh, yes, it's Welsh. But scarcely what you would call a Christian name. Ceridwen was the earth goddess, the woman in the ark of Celtic belief who became mother of the world. Everyone's true mother, the eternal all-mother, eternal because she was fired in the furnaces of creation, of earth and of under-earth, into enduring stone.' Bronwen might have been reciting from some Cymric fairy-tale or, thought Caspian, translating from memory the hypnotic cadences of ancient verse. 'She gives birth to all and devours all – makes immortal stone of fallible clay – to replenish herself and fashion those sons and daughters yet to be conceived. Men are allowed to love women of flesh whose clay will never be baked into eternity; and such women may love in return, and with their menfolk live and die because of mortal weakness. But the stone mother is the ever-lasting mother, incorruptible, impregnated only with that which makes her strong and forever impervious.'

'What poetic legends some races have invented, haven't they?' said Margaret with patronizing amusement.

'Some of Ceridwen's attributes and incarnations of the flesh,' added Bronwen thoughtfully, 'have been toned down in recent interpretations.'

'And before they were toned down, what was she?' For some reason Caspian found he was holding his breath as he waited for the answer.

'Among other things, the sow goddess.'

Now his breath snorted out. 'Sow goddess?'

'The world-mother who from stone delivers a farrow of flesh – eternity and fertility and destruction all in one. The sow who gives birth, and at one and the same time the sow who eats her young. Mortal life and death, but eternal renewal.'

Caspian glanced at Judith, her head sunk forward in a doze or a pretence of dozing. This at least was something to be thankful for: that Judith was being carried minute by minute further and further away from Ladygrove; carried to safety, to await David and then be carried yet further, on to London.

And he knew that he and Bronwen had a task to perform, whether David still expected it of them or not.

❧ 7 ❧

The cathedral tower leaned away above the mellowed bricks of the walled garden, a deep soft pink against scudding clouds. Judith sat in a sheltered corner with a rug over her knees. Here the walls retained the warmth, though as the sun went slowly round she had to move her basket chair a few inches from time to time to edge it out of the shade of the old medlar tree. Hard knots of fruit on the gnarled grey branches would be ready for picking in a few weeks' time.

A house martin soared, swooped, and settled on the sundial, twitching its tail as if it wondered whether the time had yet come to depart.

Judith turned over a page of the book on the Malayan jungle which Margaret had hoped would interest her. It all seemed remote and irrelevant, here in this secluded English garden, almost in the shadow of that very English cathedral. Yet the garden itself was also unreal. The house had an unprepossessing frontage on to a narrow lane running from the cathedral close, but showed a fine, small-scale Palladian face to the lawn. One was so tidily, comfortably enclosed here. But Judith felt only discomfort. This was not her home; nor the home she had known in London. It was simply a place where she was waiting – a junction between one line of her life and another. She was ashamed of feeling even the slightest ingratitude towards cheery, generous Margaret who had brought her here; but all she really wanted was to be taken away.

Margaret came out into the garden.

'Mrs Caspian has called to see us.' She sounded none too enthusiastic. 'I fancy she wants to make sure I haven't let you run away.'

The chair creaked as Judith pushed herself upright. It had been growing cool in that corner, and things were not much better indoors. The house had an unlived-in feel to it. It was well furnished and attractive, but one got the impression that dust covers had only recently been removed and would soon be draped back in place.

Margaret had rung for tea, though Bronwen was waving aside any intention of staying long. 'I merely thought that as I was passing I'd pay my respects and see how Judith was getting on.'

'I wasn't sure if you were still here.' Judith had in fact given it scarcely a thought. 'You decided to stay overnight, then?'

'And probably another night or two as well. It seemed a pity to neglect the opportunity of taking photographs of the city.'

Judith smiled politely. She supposed there was no reason why Bronwen should not stay on in Hereford, just like anyone else who chose to do so; yet was wary of her, obscurely troubled by the sense of both her and her husband prying, watching.

The housekeeper bustled in with a tea tray. Mrs Rodden was just the sort of kindred spirit one would have expected Margaret to engage: a bright-eyed woman with rosy cheeks and a broad smile which she kept directing at Judith – a healthy, sensible country-woman's smile saying that everything was going to be splendid, having children was splendid, today was a wonderful day and there would be many more like it.

When she had gone, Margaret poured tea for Judith and their visitor, and took over the conversation. Judith was glad to detach herself. Let there be a few conventional exchanges, a flutter of affable goodbyes, and then Bronwen would be gone and she could sink back into the quiescence of obedient waiting.

David would soon be coming for her: perhaps today, later today.

She thought of his face, and the cup and saucer in her hand rattled like chattering teeth.

But of course I don't really hate him. Can't go on hating him. It will pass.

'Are you cold, Judith?' asked Bronwen protectively.

Judith forced herself to sit quite still, apart from a shake of the head.

Margaret went to the windows and twitched the curtains an inch or so inwards along the rail. 'Too many draughts in this house. I can just hear what George will have to say when he gets here.'

'The children like their schools?' said Bronwen.

'They're settling in nicely.' Margaret would not have contemplated any other possibility.

Judith tried to envisage herself with a child – no, surely there would be two or three – who must be educated, sent away, brought home for holidays, fed and clothed and cared for. A few months ago she and David had talked at length about such matters, and laughed about them, and made and discarded a score of different plans. Now she could no longer see such a future clearly. She was not afraid, not pessimistic: just incapable of seeing what they had once foreseen.

It will pass.

'And if you don't want to leave Judith alone,' Bronwen was saying, 'I'll be delighted to come and chat. While you go shopping, or visiting the children.'

'Good heavens, there's no need to fuss over her.' Margaret was crisply dismissive. 'If I'm out, Mrs Rodden can do anything that's needed. Excellent woman, I was lucky to find her.'

'Yes, I can see that.'

Then again, when Bronwen was taking her leave and being shown out, Judith caught a few snatches from the hall: 'I don't think Judith ought to be left alone . . .' and Margaret's voice clipped and final, 'No question of being left alone . . . told you . . . Mrs Rodden's a treasure.'

Ten minutes later Judith pulled herself ponderously upstairs with the aid of the banister rail. From a small side window on the turn of the stair, probably inset into the wall for this very reason, she could peer along the lane to the gap where it met the street. Gigs, drays, coaches and the occasional bicycle flitted across the gap. Sooner or later a coach would pull up at the kerb there, and she would be fetched.

By David, of course.

Of course. Her lips formed the words, and repeated his name; but with dwindling assurance.

'Not if it means exposing you to dangers within Judith again,' said Caspian gruffly.

'I hoped you'd have recovered from those suspicions. If we're really intended to protect Judith – '

'What about your own protection? I won't risk you.'

'You're still jealous.'

'I won't risk you,' he said again, fiercely. 'If you can stay reasonably close to Judith without making Margaret too irate, well and good. But you are not to let yourself be drawn into the maze of her mind. You hear me?'

'Yes,' she said with grudging submissiveness, 'I hear you.'

'Then you also hear that I love you.'

She stood at the window of the hotel looking down on the busy street, and put out one hand to him. He came beside her, and their fingertips played together. 'Yes,' she said, this time without grudging a breath of it, 'I hear you.'

Twenty yards along the street from The Green Dragon they could just make out the entrance to the lane which went past Mrs Henderson's front door. Bronwen remembered her own reluctance, half an hour ago, to leave that door: to leave Judith.

'But what *is* the danger?' she fretted. 'She can hardly be spirited away – or drawn back despite herself, as I was to Hexney?'

That she would never forget. Its terrors had been overcome with this man beside her, this man who was now, blessedly, her husband; overcome by the strength of his mind after she had been remorselessly called back to the Fenland village which she had wanted never to see again. Life with him, love with him, had driven those terrors out and kept them at bay. But she would never forget.

Caspian said: 'I don't think Lady Brobury, or whatever power works through her, has the psychic strength to reach out like that, over that distance.'

'Then unless she sends her swineherd, or he comes of his own accord – '

'I can't see him getting much of a welcome on Margaret's doorstep!'

They laughed. In broad daylight, above a busy Hereford street, the thought of the outraged Margaret and the lumpish Morris meeting again face to face could be funny. So quickly did the past lose its menace.

Bronwen made herself think back to Lady Brobury and see her again, as she might have been in a photograph taken from its correct, numbered file. It was difficult to see her as a conscious villainess. But simply by sitting there in that lodge of hers, resentful and self-engrossed, she could ill-wish others, direct her spite at them, as village crones and would-be witches had done for centuries.

And allow her swineherd to kill her husband . . . or will him to do so?

The perspective shifted and distorted.

'I have an appointment,' said Caspian, 'at the cathedral library. Would you care to stroll along with me?'

Crossing the quadrangle of the cathedral close they both glanced automatically at the other end of the lane. In that huddle of tiled roofs and intersecting walls it was difficult to tell which, if any, were the garden walls and roof of the house where Judith was staying. Then they were under the great bulk of the cathedral, with the bishop's palace overlooking the river beyond. Up-river were high, clustering woods; and far off against the sky the familiar silhouette of the Black Mountains.

The library opened from a cloister connecting the bishop's palace with the cathedral. Inside, the dank stony smell of the cloister was replaced by the mixed aroma of old paper and parchment, leather, and varnished woodwork.

The archivist was a residentiary canon who, in spite of confirming that Dr Caspian had indeed made an appointment, was cautious about committing himself to any guarantee of producing specific documents.

'I am not quite sure, doctor, what you're seeking. As you'll doubtless realize, many of our treasures have to be handled with the greatest care, not exposed to the light for too long, and not studied for – mm – purposes inimical to ecclesiastical precepts.'

'I'm searching,' said Caspian, 'for records of religious foundations associated with Mockblane and Ladygrove Manor.'

'Ah. The Broburys.' The canon sounded even more doubtful. 'You know the family?'

'We have recently been staying with Sir David.'

'Yes, yes. I have not yet had the pleasure of meeting him. I did have occasional contacts with his father.' The bluish lips quirked slightly. 'A bon vivant, Sir Mortimer.'

'We've only known Sir David.'

'Mm. Yes. Well, Dr Caspian, we do have some church documents from Mockblane, and some reports submitted to various bishops. I'm afraid the collection is incomplete, however.'

'Destroyed at the Reformation?' guessed Caspian.

'Not all, by no means. There were the usual losses, naturally. But many monasteries and other foundations entrusted their records into faithful hands. And once the first wave of demolition was over, the Church of England naturally wished to preserve and respect the historical evidences of its . . . ah . . . predecessors.'

'Still you say your collection is incomplete.'

'There are some items which we know to exist but which we cannot reclaim for the library. Many attempts have been made, but . . . well, frankly, the situation is an odd one. At one time and another, especially when Puritan zealots had the upper hand, there were attempts to seize and destroy records which it was felt were best expunged from the face of the earth.'

'Because of some contentious point of religious usage?'

'Some murmured blasphemy. Others of deviations which were best kept from all save the most incorruptible scholars.'

'But you know where this missing material is.'

'Some of it,' said the canon reluctantly, 'is in the hands of an eccentric living some miles away, outside Madley.'

'An eccentric?'

'Not a churchgoer.' The austere condemnation rang above the rows of books and died away into their dusty bindings.

'Then why should he wish to preserve such documents?'

'They came into the hands of his family when, it has to be admitted, they might otherwise have been destroyed by some rather too fervent ascetics. In spite of repeated pleas for their lodgement in our safe keeping, they have not been offered to the library. And you'll appreciate how difficult it is to make an issue of it, when, without that family's intervention, they would probably not be in existence by now.'

'What chance would there be of my inspecting these items?'

'I would suggest, doctor, that you first study what we have in our

149

own archives. Then you may decide how far you still wish to pursue the matter.'

Caspian kissed Bronwen. 'If I'm permitted, I can see myself busy here for a few hours. I'll see you at the hotel, later. And . . .'

'Yes,' she smiled, 'I did hear you.'

She left him to walk on between the high bookcases with their dangling chains, each chain securing some priceless volume, while she went out again into the chill cloister and on into the fresh air.

There was ample time for her to collect her camera from the hotel and take a few pictures of the riverside, the bridge, and the cathedral precincts before the light became too insipid.

It was almost dark when Caspian returned. Clearly he had enjoyed himself tracking down references to the religious history of Mock-blane, Ladygrove and their valley. 'But the gaps are formidable. Surviving records tell the story much as we've already heard it. But there are some odd references that die on one – like going along a lane, turning the corner, and finding that the lane has come to a dead end. Or, rather, that it peters out when you know that it ought to continue.'

'So you're going to see the eccentric at Madley tomorrow.'

'How did you know?'

'You have a mind,' she said solemnly, 'like an open book.'

'All I can say at the moment is that I have a lot more books to open before I can establish the definitive text.'

'And this eccentric character will open them to you?'

'The question, too, is open. He may not even admit me. But Canon Westering has given me a few tips on how to worm my way into his good graces.'

'A cunning fellow, your canon.'

'Still not cunning enough to reclaim those records for his library.'

'And what you've learnt so far . . .?'

'I've told you – too many gaps.'

'But the solid ground between the gaps must give you some idea of the terrain.'

Caspian hesitated, then said: 'Enough to make me suspect some worrying truths behind the traditions. If Judith were still at Lady-grove I'd be much more worried.'

'Because if she gave birth there – '

'Then,' said Caspian, 'I believe the curse and the house and the Brobury line would at last have come together again.'

The carriage drew up across the end of the lane. The coachman got down and opened the door, putting up a gloved hand to help his mistress step down. From the window on the stairs Judith watched Lady Brobury tug at a crumpled pleat in her skirt and then walk regally towards the house, seemingly hardly to need even a confirmatory glance at the other doors and numbers she passed.

Walking smartly in the opposite direction, Mrs Rodden was setting off with a shopping basket of closely plaited straw.

Judith went downstairs, timing her descent so that she had reached the bottom step just as the doorbell rang.

Margaret crossed the narrow hall and opened the door.

'Mother! I wasn't expecting you. I thought perhaps – '

'Perhaps it would be David?' Lady Brobury walked in and nodded companionably at Judith, whom she had manifestly expected to find in exactly that position.

'I did think it was time he got here.' Margaret looked over her mother's shoulder; but there was nobody following.

'Oh, dear. I'm afraid there has been . . . an incident.'

Judith felt a throb, a missed beat and then somehow an extra beat, in her breast; and an answering throb in her stomach.

Margaret closed the door and said spikily: 'You're not going to say there has been another accident to the carriage, or the roof has collapsed with the beetle, or the church has been attacked again?'

'There's no use talking to David. He won't listen. And now look what has happened.'

'What has happened?'

'His ankle. He got so angry, storming about the place rounding up those who had damaged the church, that he stepped into some hole or other and twisted his ankle. It will be days before he can move about properly. So I came in his place' – she smiled at Judith – 'to fetch you home.'

They went on into a room overlooking the garden. Margaret paused in the doorway and called along the passage: 'Mrs Rodden!'

'I saw her go out shopping,' said Judith.

Lady Brobury settled herself in a chair by the window. 'A not altogether disagreeable place, Margaret,' she conceded. 'But lacking any distinctive quality, wouldn't you say?'

Margaret said: 'Mother, I don't think there's any question of Judith going back to Ladygrove. I haven't gone to all the trouble of bringing her here simply in order to despatch her back again.'

'She should be with her husband.'

'In her present condition she can hardly wait on him. And I'm sure he wouldn't expect it.'

Margaret's brusqueness drew none of the plaintive retorts which might have been expected from her mother. Lady Brobury, wearing a mauve pleated skirt and pelisse mantle, her spoon bonnet garnished with opaque white beads like mistletoe berries, looked very calm and sure of herself. Her expression told Judith that all was well and they would not have to wait much longer.

Margaret glanced dubiously from one to the other.

Smoothly Judith asked: 'And Mr Goswell? Has he recovered from that outrage?'

'Or has he twisted his ankle also?' snapped Margaret scornfully.

Lady Brobury shrugged. 'Quite incompetent, poor man. Quite unable to cope.'

Her gloved hand rose a mere fraction of an inch to sketch a dismissive gesture. Mr Goswell, it appeared, was discarded. He had served whatever purpose she had needed him for, and now was of no further significance.

She went on, with a slight, enquiring turn of her head: 'And those strange friends of David's – the Caspians? They caught their train in good time?'

'I fancy they're still here,' said Margaret.

'In Hereford?' There was the faintest tautening of Lady Brobury's neck muscles.

'They decided to stay on a day or two and take a few photographs.'

'A very irregular way of life. I confess I never took to the pair. I know they were acquaintances of David's, but . . . upon my word, a stage conjuror with more time on his hands than seems good for him, and a young married woman playing about with those camera contraptions . . .! No, I was glad to see the back of them.'

'They were a great help to me,' Margaret reminded her.

'Oh, that nonsense.'

'David was going to have it out with that dreadful Morris man – '

'David now has a dozen other things to deal with,' said her mother, 'and a twisted ankle into the bargain.'

Judith saw her mother-in-law tilt strangely sideways. The room shook, then spun round. She clutched the arm of her chair. From somewhere she heard Margaret's voice. Then it was Lady Brobury's: 'Yes, I thought she must be very near her time.' And then the room steadied, but pain lanced through her. She let go of the chair and pressed both hands on to her stomach.

'It's started?'

Margaret was on her feet.

'I thought so,' said Lady Brobury happily. 'Now, there is plenty of time. It will take its own good time.'

Margaret turned to the door. 'Mrs Rodden . . .' She let out a gasp of exasperation. 'There's no telling how long she will take to get back.'

Her mother was smiling equably.

Judith felt pain recede like an ebbing tide, and longed to sing her thankfulness. But there was the consciousness of the waves building up again, far out; and even before they struck again she felt the tremor of their coming. Yet there was a long, long wait between the spasms. In that waiting period, Lady Brobury sat with her hands in her lap, watching her with an affection that Judith had not seen in her eyes before.

Margaret made up her mind. 'I shall fetch the midwife. And let Dr Hadfield know, in case we have to call on him. Very reliable man. Had him in to the children when we got here.'

'Yes, dear,' said Lady Brobury. 'Perhaps it would be wise. But don't run about too wildly. There are hours to go yet.'

Judith braced herself for a pang which failed to come.

'I'll be back just as soon as I can.' Margaret squeezed her shoulder, and hurried off.

When they heard the front door slam behind her, Lady Brobury shook her head gently. 'Such a fuss. Hours to go, my dear. Hours. But I think we ought to be on our way.'

Judith looked full into that inviting, reassuring face. She had been expecting this and had known the hour must come, but still some other part of her struggled to deny it. There were surely other things, other people to take into account. There had been Sir Mortimer. *You won't bring yourselves to Ladygrove before the child is born.* And David had been insistent on sending her away. Because he had been told to insist? She seemed, too, to hear an echo of Bronwen's voice in the hall: *I don't think Judith ought to be left alone* . . .

But I am not alone.

Lady Brobury said: 'The carriage is waiting. I knew we should soon need it.'

'But Margaret will be coming back with the midwife. She'll be expecting me to – '

'You must come home.'

'Perhaps if we wait, and explain to Margaret?'

'What is there to explain,' asked Lady Brobury mildly, 'that she could possibly understand?' She waited a moment, then leaned forward. The folds and creases of her face, the dewlap and the puckered lines, all seemed to have hardened and set into a stony mould; and her eyes were like glistening, inset stones. 'Your child cannot be born here. This is nowhere.'

'There's no time for me to – '

'There is time. Comfortable time. Nothing is prepared, here. At home, all is prepared. It has been fashioned over a long, long time, all for this day.'

There was a wrench inside which robbed Judith of breath. Soundlessly she opened her mouth wide. And Lady Brobury went on relentlessly:

'It is better for you to face it now and lift the curse from the family. The men have no power to do it. It is for a woman – for the mother. The folly of the past was the Brobury flight from their ancestral home, not their presence in it. And the damage was done above all to their womenfolk, the women they married and who bore their children. And will be done again! It will happen again and again

154

until one woman has the courage to bear her child at Ladygrove and offer him back.'

'Offer him back – to *what*?'

Again Judith was tormented by the urge to draw away; but it was as vain as the attempt to retreat from the slow, pitiless waves of pain.

'There will be more children, later. Children you may keep. But if your firstborn enters the world away from his rightful home, he will bring unhappiness to his women, and to his son and his son's sons. Generation after generation will be plagued by the sins of the far past. So come home, my dear.'

Lady Brobury had risen from her chair and was holding out her right hand. Judith reached for it and allowed herself to be helped slowly up.

'And afterwards?' she said in a trance.

'It will be ended and you will know true happiness. And for your son the thread will be snapped and he can never know unhappiness.'

'A boy. It's to be a boy.'

'Oh, yes,' said Lady Brobury, 'tonight you will be delivered of a son.'

Traffic at the junction of Broad Street and High Street had tangled itself to a standstill. Only a few smaller vehicles could edge round the corner, often running a wheel up along the kerb. Bronwen, coming away from an admiring inspection of the old butchers' guildhall, made three attempts to cross the road between the muddle of vehicles, but was driven back by an erratically steered bicycle and then by two sprightly bays.

At last she could risk another attempt. She had reached the far side before something drew her attention to a brougham which was beginning slowly to ease its way out of the confusion. There was something familiar about it. She had travelled in it. Startled, she raised her eyes in time to see a face drifting back from the window into the privacy of the interior. It had been Lady Brobury's face: she was sure of it.

Bronwen tried to wave, to call out. She took one step back into the gutter, and narrowly escaped plunging under the wheels of an accelerating van.

It could have been nobody else but Lady Brobury.

Bronwen quickened her pace. Gathering up her skirts, she was almost running as she reached the entrance to the lane. She had to slow down in order to let two other women precede her; and saw that one of them was Margaret Henderson.

Margaret recognized her in the same moment. 'Oh, Mrs Caspian.' She did not pause, but talked over her shoulder as she approached her front door. 'I'm afraid this is not a good time for visiting. Judith's labour has begun.'

'If I can help – '

'Thank you, no. You've been most kind, and I'm grateful for what you did for *me*, but I don't think you should concern yourself further with us.'

'I . . . has Lady Brobury been here today?'

'She's still here.' Margaret opened the door. 'Of that I'm sure.'

She hurried her companion in ahead of her, and was about to close the door when she saw the trouble in Bronwen's face.

'Really, Mrs Caspian, I did say – '

'Please,' said Bronwen. 'Let me see Judith. Just for a moment.'

'There is absolutely no need – '

'Which room, madam?' The woman who had gone in, shedding her coat to disclose a crisp blue dress and starched collar, turned back across the hall.

'That door on the left.'

'There's nobody in there, madam. I've just looked.'

'Perhaps mother has helped her up to the bedroom.' Margaret went to the foot of the stairs. 'Mother? Judith?' When the only answer was silence she began to climb.

Bronwen stepped inside the still open front door.

'Don't you realize,' she cried, 'that Judith has been taken back?'

'Taken back where?'

'To Ladygrove.'

'What utter nonsense. Why on earth would . . .' Margaret looked up towards the landing. 'Mother, are you there?'

'I tell you they're on their way to Ladygrove.'

Bronwen wanted to turn and run, to find Caspian, to set out in pursuit with him. But he was too far away. Desperately she opened her mind and tried to summon him, but among the thousand deafening noises which crowded in there was no whisper of his voice. All she heard clearly was the sound of what he had said yesterday, more direct and ominous now.

The curse and the house and the Brobury line were at last coming together again.

PART III

The Offering

From the cloistered hush of Hereford's chained library to the clutter of Mr Enoch Vaughan's study was a considerable leap, but Caspian found himself enjoying one setting as much as the other. They had in common an atmosphere of musty detachment, of erudition for erudition's sake, which put all the turmoil of the everyday world into its correct and pitiable proportion. At such times Caspian was tempted to consider early retirement so that he might devote more time to academic pastimes: not a complete withdrawal, but at least a transfer from the mundane to the metaphysical. Nostalgically he remembered the pleasures of youthful scholastic application in London, Heidelberg and Prague, when even the most gruelling academic tasks seemed to allow one all the time in the world, and everything was new and exalting. There had been so much to read, so much to learn, so many concepts to fit together into philosophical unity, and so many golden moments of intellectual revelation. Now the days and years raced past too swiftly. There was no time for research or meditation. One had learnt too much, lived too fast, yet still knew too little.

And all the while, as men played verbal games with their religions and languages and superstitions, the unknowable was crawling through swamps of black sortilege, awaiting the call to lift a foul head and engulf the damned, the foolish, and the unwary innocent.

Turning over Enoch Vaughan's papers and trying to shut out most of Vaughan's spasmodic bursts of monologue, Caspian smiled rue-fully to himself. Of course he would never now adapt to the academic life. Even in those younger days he had, to be honest, spent com-paratively little time in that cherished seclusion. Remembering books and dissertations, he remembered also the duels at Heidelberg, the horses and gambling at Pardubitz, and the sleight of hand which he had practised so assiduously until it became a flamboyant party piece and ultimately his profession. He would never be capable of abandoning the worldly, histrionic Count Caspar entirely for the earnest Dr Caspian. The two were one and must work side by side. Offered a challenge in the unpredictable, untidy, ungovernable outside world, he would rarely be able to resist picking up the gauntlet – whether the challenge was that of discrediting mediumistic fakers or of confronting with his telepathic powers the threats of worldly and other-worldly chaos.

It was so agreeable to turn over documents and yellowing tomes, alert for the authentic nuances of history, piecing together the mysteries of the past with no urgent need to relate them to present exigencies. But he could never permanently immure himself within some academic sanctuary.

The thought of immurement brought him back to the crabbed lettering on the pages he was slowly turning over.

Enoch Vaughan said: 'You see – how the ancient truths have been perverted by these clerical sycophants, you see? Oh, the shameful falsehoods they're capable of! Shameful, every word of it. You're with me, I'm sure?'

Vaughan was a shrunken little man of about seventy, with a disproportionately large head and an expansive, flowing white beard. His eyes under a mop of white hair were like bright jet, darting and sparkling and querulous. He had received Caspian with the most courteous suspicion; denied the existence of any papers on the Mockblane matter whatsoever; then denied the right of anyone else to inspect them or the worthiness of anyone to attempt an understanding which only he could achieve; and then thawed as Caspian slipped in an anti-clerical joke which the canon had obligingly told him would go down well, and added a reference to his own Welsh wife, who was the seventh daughter of a seventh daughter.

'Ah, then you'll be one who understands, won't you?' Vaughan's head was quizzically cocked to one side. 'Sort of one of us, like?'

Now, disgorging one chest of scrolls, parchments and books after another, scrabbling and digging out a folio here, a package there, he talked in fits and starts irrespective of what stage Caspian had attained in his reading.

'A poor, ignorant peasant girl,' he was ranting on, 'sold into the bondage of a wicked church for the sake of her wretched family's prestige . . . unctuous hypocrites . . . a child who might have known the old natural truths, sacrificed to the miseries of the new falsehood. Christianity!' said Mr Vaughan with all the severity of a Methodist minister condemning the devil and all his works. 'A shallow mask created by cowards to disguise the face of truth.'

The sonorous condemnations came oddly from that mild, generous face swathed in its shimmering patriarchal mane. From time to time Caspian looked up and nodded politely, while fitting together the fragments he had unearthed in Hereford and trying to relate them to the uncatalogued relics preserved by Enoch Vaughan. As a pattern began at last to emerge, and he saw how his theories were over-shadowed by the immediate reality, Caspian began to worry.

But Judith was safe. He had time to browse; time to conjecture what dangers she had escaped.

From the cartularies and bishops' registers in Hereford cathedral library he had winnowed a number of references to the original church of St Alkmund, including mention of the anchoress Matilda. But these did little more than record her arrival, list pious donations during a number of years, and then state baldly that she had been absolved from her vows. There was no documentation of her appeal to the bishop for release, or of his formal declaration. It was not too surprising: medieval records tended to be sketchy, and many could have been scattered or destroyed over the centuries.

More substantial documentation came with the endowment of a Carmelite priory by a Sir Henry Brobury, granting use of the existing church as a cornerstone of the conventual buildings, while another church was built for the laity on the other side of the river.

The priory buildings enshrined the cell of the dead Matilda. A register from the priory scriptorium made early reference to the protection of her holy relics, but in very formal language. Later, all mention ceased. If there had been any actual physical relics, they could have been destroyed at the Reformation or taken away, as so many objects of veneration were secretly taken away by monks and nuns fleeing to the protection of Continental houses or into hiding in their own country.

What did come across consistently was a strong sense of mission:

the duty of guardianship, never relaxed. The devout attendants of St Edmund or St Thomas à Becket could not have been more rigorous than these austere sisters in their watch over the cell of the anchoress Matilda of Mockblane, who had gone out into the world but returned to her final immurement. But whereas St Edmundsbury and Canterbury had welcomed pilgrims to their shrines, the nuns of Mockblane not only shunned the world themselves but kept people away from the anchoress's cell.

On some pages of their cartulary were a few disturbing passages, one of them supplemented by a loose copy of an actual letter from the prioress. She reported to the mother abbey on the illness of a sister who had asked to spend a night of devotion in the cell. It seemed that the young woman had been feverish for more than a week, seeing visions of devils and crying for a mother who did not, as far as could be gathered from her ravings, resemble her own mother. Not long after, a novice died from an unspecified ailment; but it was mentioned that she had disobediently strayed unattended into the cell.

At no stage was it ever suggested that the cell itself should be demolished.

The wording of one of the sisterhood's vows, given a full page to itself and more elaborately lettered and illuminated than the rest, was strange: 'We vow eternal watchfulness against what lies below, that it may not again rise within our walls or our souls.'

Caspian mentally set that alongside another line he had recently pondered over. *Pray for deliverance from Matilda . . . thrust back in for her own good.*

There were two missives to a fourteenth-century bishop, and part of his reply to one of them. Some nuns wished to leave the convent and the order, and return to the world. Three were allowed to do so, but evidently only after long examination and prayer and heart-searching. It was stipulated by the bishop that they must live far away and speak nothing of their experiences and never return to this part of the country. One who wished to remain within the order but begged she should be freed from this priory was sent to France, and there was a reference to 'instructions' being given to her new mother superior. No further word was ever recorded of those who had left.

The story came to a brutal end with the fell phrases of the order of expropriation, and the Royal Commissioner's report confirming that this had been carried out. After all the altar furnishings, the priory bell and roof leading had been removed by the Crown, the property was handed back to the Broburys. It was here that the commissioner recorded the 'intemperate and irreligious conduct of the woman but lately prioress of this house, who did not only refuse the dole and comforts offered by His most generous Majesty our Sovereign Lord the King, but did cry out a curse upon the most worthy family by whose grace her very house was founded and maintained'. The wording of the curse was as Caspian had already heard it from the lips of David Brobury:

> Strife shall be 'twixt man and wife
> Till yielded back there be the life
> Of thy house's first-born son.

Knowing more of the background now, Caspian found it odd that the prioress, however dismayed by her ejection into the perils of the outer world, should have directed her wrath at the Broburys rather than at the king and his commissioners. True that the family had wavered in its religious allegiance; but it would have been of no advantage to her if they had remained faithful.

As he lifted the chained volume back into its slot on the shelf, the canon observed: 'There is another version of the Brobury curse, incidentally, in the Lambeth Palace library in London.'

'Another version?'

'The wording itself is little changed. But the circumstances of its delivery are different. According to that other report, the prioress seemed to one witness to be quoting rather than voicing the malediction herself. It is agreed that she was distraught, and much of what she cried was lost: but this interpretation suggests that she warned of the ills which would befall if the pious guardians of the site were driven away, and *reminded* them – if it meant anything to any of them – of an ancient curse. She was recalling ancient vindictiveness, not voicing her own.'

'But this one' – Caspian tapped the spine of the book – 'is the preferred version?'

'Preferred and disseminated by Henry VIII and his minions,' said the archivist, 'to help in the campaign of discrediting those whose religious houses they had seized.'

Caspian thought of the dedicated woman's despair as her words fell on deaf ears. Could she simply wash her hands of responsibility and walk away? Or, like her predecessors, guardians of the anchoress's cell and its secrets, had her sense of vocation remained so strong that even after death she could not allow herself to abandon the task? He thought of that spirit resonating on the air of Ladygrove, of a devotion so strong that down the centuries it watched over the site – shielding any Brobury wife from the cell and its environs when she was pregnant, preferring the Brobury curse to continue from generation to generation rather than open the way to an ending infinitely, hideously worse . . .

And now that phantom guardian, which had striven to prevent the 'offering back', had been dismissed by the inept Goswell and his far more powerful manipulator, Lady Brobury.

The canon was looking lovingly along his rows of books. Caspian said: 'You mentioned having known Sir Mortimer. Did he ever consult you about his family history?'

'Sir Mortimer was not a scholarly man. Our meetings were purely fortuitous. He lived more by . . . well, shall we say his instincts?'

Yes, thought Caspian dourly. By his instincts and appetites. Yet at least his instinct had told him to keep David and Judith away from Ladygrove at a crucial time. Even if Sir Mortimer had not been interested in the documentation of the Brobury curse, he believed in some aspects of it.

With all these speculations shuffling and readjusting in his mind, Caspian began to insert what he could glean from Enoch Vaughan's contributions.

One of the more important was a story bearing on the menacing elements of the Matilda cult. A nun released at the time of the Dissolution claimed that she had wished to leave earlier but had been prevented and cruelly disciplined by the prioress. She had been forbidden her freedom on the grounds that she would be a gossip and a mischief-maker. Now she had her revenge by proving how well-founded this judgment of her had been. Many of the nuns were mocked as they emerged from their years of seclusion; but because of her readiness to denounce the prioress she was sheltered by one of Thomas Cromwell's men. There was an intimation, impossible to verify after three and a half centuries, that she might have married him; or she could have been, if only briefly, his mistress. Her story was written down by one of Cromwell's scribes, then lost, then rediscovered and added to Enoch Vaughan's collection. It could have been an outpouring of pure malice, forced from her or distorted by her own spiteful imagination. Or it could have been true.

If it were true, it tended to confirm the evidence that guardianship of the anchoress's cell was not in devotion to a sacred memory but as a stern duty to keep others safe from what had been unleashed within. The anchoress Matilda had, according to this version, been released from her cell without due investigation of her motives, and once free had behaved so shamefully and practised such abominations that it had been necessary to recapture her. It was rumoured that she had fled into the hills to join acolytes of the old religion there, had been made one with them and the villagers who still in secret worshipped the ancients, and had been got with child. It was the lord of the manor who finally trapped her and returned her for final imprisonment and repentance. 'And she did curse most abominably then and thereafter, and call down wickedness and revile the godly, until her voice wearied and was stilled forever by our most merciful Lord.'

There was no mention of the Broburys in all that cursing. But such mention would have won no favour with those who, like the Broburys, had supported Henry VIII and been rewarded with property and monastic riches.

Out of remembered nightmare Caspian saw David Brobury's face descending on the girl writhing in the grass. She had burned with unholy joy in the ravishment; but if she had mothered his child and then been thrust back again into her solitude, well might she have cursed him and all who came after him.

With a dry throat he said: 'What happened to the child?'

'Oh, you've reached that bit, have you?' Vaughan bowed his massive head over the page. 'Yes, one wonders, of course one wonders. It may have been taken away and brought up elsewhere.

Left for the priests in the hills to care for. Or . . . disposed of by the poor girl's persecutors.'

A firstborn Brobury, disposed of like a superfluous kitten?

If a wrongdoer escapes them, they will even slaughter the innocent. Again he was reminded of Julius Caesar's words. *If a human life is not given for a human life, the gods cannot be appeased.*

He said: 'You speak of the priests in the hills. And you've referred more than once to the old truths. How far down into these valleys did those . . . those truths reach?'

Vaughan chuckled gleefully. 'There now, you do know. Didn't I say you'd be one who'd understand?'

Of course the Celts had slyly pursued their old ways and worshipped their old gods, and in secret there had been enclaves of Druid priests long after the Romans had thought them exterminated. Christians had built over the old pagan sites, sometimes adopting features of the old religion to incorporate in their own, sometimes striving to nullify such survivals by setting their own altars atop the ancient ones. But in those consecrated stones there might linger something too mighty for suppression by new prayers, new rituals – like a mammoth preserved in ice, waiting to be released, resurrected from the heart of the solid prison.

He said bluntly: 'Was the anchoress's cell, to your knowledge, on the site of some old Druid holy place?'

'Yes, you do know.'

'So that was what terrified the girl out of her wits. And terrified those charged with looking after the storm centre once she had been destroyed.'

'Destroyed!' cried Vaughan indignantly. 'It was not the old ones who destroyed her, but the wicked usurpers. If she cursed before they walled her in and left her, it was not the folk of the old persuasion she cursed, but the new sects which brought guilt and bitterness to our ancient lands. The Christians denied the oak and the ash, perverted the meaning of the mistletoe, defiled the places they stole.'

The shrillness of it suggested a fanaticism which could turn violent. In the closing years of this materialistic century Caspian had encountered a score of perverse cults and a thousand unstable practitioners of ill-conceived rites in shabby back rooms and gas-lit meeting halls; had depressingly explored down too many contaminated streets and alleys. But Enoch Vaughan, in spite of his fervour, did not belong with the shabby sorcerers. He was one of the romantics, substituting daydreams of ancient splendour for drab reality. There were those who equated the Druids with the sages of Persia and India; and those cranks who swore that their fanciful invented rituals were inspired by the arcane precepts of Druid Britain. Harmless – provided the poetic daydreams were all.

'But praise be,' Vaughan was saying, 'they never really left, you know: the old ones never actually went away.'

Carefully Caspian ventured: 'But suppose Matilda the anchoress didn't understand that? She had been schooled in other beliefs.'

'Barbarities!'

'Suppose that for her, an innocent in spite of all she may have gone through, the horrors were not those of ecclesiastical punishment but of Celtic echoes still pulsating in her cell? That to her the ultimate terror was to be thrust back into the one place she knew to be devil-ridden with old beliefs which were anathema to all she had been taught?'

'What could there possibly be on that ancient site but sweetness and tranquillity? These monstrous tales of – '

'Ceridwen!' Caspian knew he was being unwise, but the day was drawing on and he wished to be finished. 'The sow goddess – how can you fit her into a pantheon of sweet, enriching beliefs?'

'Barbarous! Ceridwen, the goddess of spring and the corn, of rebirth and renewal.' Vaughan stood up. 'You are not the man I thought you. I have been deceived.'

'I'm sorry, but as a scholar yourself you must surely know the different incarnations of – '

'Take your slanders elsewhere.'

Vaughan was scooping up papers and books, shovelling them willy-nilly into the nearest open box.

'Thank you for your patience,' Caspian said, too late. 'You've been most helpful. I wouldn't want you to think – '

'I was right not to entrust my secrets to those Hereford blasphemers. Wrong to let you misinterpret them with your impious eyes.' Vaughan began edging Caspian towards the door. It was clear that he had no intention of shaking hands. At the door he declaimed: 'You will learn, when it is too late. You will all of you learn, when it is too late. The old ones . . . they never left.'

Caspian would have been glad of his wife's company on the journey back to Hereford. There were so many points to be discussed – so many which would have stung a sharp, stimulating response from her.

'Lady Brobury.' He said it in an undertone, questioning, as if the mere name would provoke an answer.

It might be that the old woman was not entirely responsible for all that had happened and been meant to happen. But without her the tide of evil might not have found a channel. Evil does not flourish on its own, in a vacuum. It needs an Aeolian harp through which to breathe and make itself heard: without instruments tuned to the right resonance it cannot play its fearsome tunes. If human beings are not ready for evil, it cannot take on substance.

By peevishness and a growing spitefulness, by willing injury and then death, Lady Brobury had opened herself to forces which now possessed her and would use her. No longer scraping disjointedly at a few petty resentments, she had been taken over by a vast hellish symphony which she was no longer capable of directing. She, not it, was being directed now.

But all to no purpose. The theme of that infernal music would not be heard by the destined victim. Judith, thought Caspian with renewed thankfulness, was out of range, out of hearing.

❧ 2 ❧

David Brobury lay in a drugged sleep, his arms sprawling slack on the counterpane and his lips parted half an inch or so. Margaret spoke to him, shook his elbow, and spoke more sharply; but he was too deeply blanketed by the miasma of some potion to hear or be commanded back to wakefulness.

She glared round at the butler. 'Whatever was he given to put him in this state?'

'I couldn't be saying, Miss Margaret. It was her ladyship – Lady Charlotte, that is – was tending to him.'

Bronwen said urgently: 'Where are they now – the two ladies?'

'They . . . went out into the grounds, ma'am.'

'*Where* in the grounds?'

'It was my impression, ma'am, they went walking down towards the stream.'

Bronwen turned towards the door. Behind her, Margaret said: 'Whatever this nonsense may mean, Jephson, I think you had better accompany us. And perhaps bring one of the footmen.'

'I'm afraid we couldn't be doing that, miss . . . er, begging your pardon, ma'am, I mean.'

'I don't know what you do mean, Jephson.'

'We don't want no part in anything that's going on, that's what. Bad enough last time, all them goings-on up and down stairs. But out there . . . no, that'd be ten times worse.'

Bronwen did not hear Margaret's reply. She was in too much of a hurry to be out of the house and on Judith's trail. Then Margaret was panting indignantly after her.

'What has got into this place?'

Bronwen said: 'Go back to David. Stay with him.'

'I'll do no such thing. Where's Judith? Where's mother? What do they think they're playing at, at this time of night, out here in – '

'Go back to David. I'll try to save Judith.'

'Save her? What are all these mystifications of yours, Mrs Caspian? Really, you're as bad as my mother.'

'I hope not,' said Bronwen soberly.

She could not delay in argument with Margaret. The time was approaching, and she must face Judith's dangers with her. There was nobody else to help: nobody now but herself, nothing but the strength which she alone could summon.

The slope down to the footbridge was frosted by a faint starshine. Even without this pallid illumination Bronwen could have trod surefootedly to the edge of the stream and the end of the bridge. She was guided by the sound of Judith's mind, now at the entrance to the maze.

Margaret brushed past her, less sure of her footing but determined to take charge. 'I think this is a family matter, Mrs Caspian.'

She had one hand on the rail of the bridge when light gleamed faintly on four smooth, sharp tusks at the other end. Two sentinel hogs with dipped heads waited to tear at any intruder. And from beyond, from the grove and from' within the woven yew hedges of the maze, there came a slow, harsh rustling like ripples over shingle: the restless snuffling and prowling of the hungry, waiting herd.

Margaret took a courageous step forward. There was a threatening grunt, and the bridge swayed.

'Morris! Are you in there? I warn you – if you don't come out at once and move these beasts, it'll be the worse for you.'

It was vain, grotesque: the cry of social discipline, of well-ordered normality, into the heart of seething primordial chaos.

'Go back,' Bronwen commanded fiercely. 'I can do nothing with you here. Go *back*! The servants know what they're talking about.'

She was so compelling that Margaret retreated. When Bronwen settled herself on the damp grass as close as she could get to the edge of the stream barring her from the grove, there was an instant in which Margaret was about to try a last protest. Then she backed slowly away, a forlorn, bewildered shadow against the shadowy hulk of the house.

Bronwen crossed her wrists over her knees. She closed her eyes and let consciousness of Margaret, the slope and the gardens and the house drain away. Picturing the stream a few inches below, she let everything else trickle over the bank into it.

And then, when her mind was cleared of all sight and memory and sensation, she began to draw in awareness of the grove, the maze ... and Judith, and what was living and throbbing in Judith.

All at once it came in a flood: all the past in one stunning cataract, so that she was battered and thrown about and in danger of drowning. She was no longer pacing out a succession of steps from the past, sharing spasmodic flashes of pain and love and despair. In a few seconds she knew and was Matilda, knowing and reaching out for the physical anguish of creation and re-creation. As Judith knew, and accepted.

Pain stabbed. Bronwen felt her own womb racked by it. She carried a child, felt it struggling to be born, longed to deliver it and hold it briefly in her arms.

Briefly, because it must be delivered again: offered back.

So it must be. She remembered what had been done and knew what now had to be done.

She remembered all.

I remember my cell and the cold which became heat, and the fear which became fire, and what it taught me about myself and the things beyond myself. Though what I was taught made little reason until the teachers in the hills took me in and taught me so much more.

Yet this is not memory. It is as real and present as it ever was. I am what I always was and shall be so until my defilers are brought down and do at last yield up what I enjoined upon them.

The mother waits for me. I, the mortal mother, shall offer back to the eternal mother what was stolen from me and so from her. This time the gods shall be appeased.

Pain is a knife through me. And again, and again. So much torment within my body before I deliver the son who will be spared all save a few seconds of the pain of living.

I remember the tearing of my flesh by the father, as more shall now be torn by the son.

The man is with me again, in me again. I hate the despoilment but yearn for it again. He laughs because he is happy to have been proven right.

'Truly it was a lie, my fair.' He is handsome, and swaggering, and laughs again when I drag my torn habit down about the ravages he has wrought on me. 'You did indeed have a taste for a man.'

'You have treated me most shamefully.' It is true, yet he is right to shake that fine head of his and go on smiling in those fine Brobury eyes of his.

'I will find you a place to rest.' He says it gently enough now that the blaze of his passion has died away, and offers me his hand as a gentleman would offer it to the gentlest lady of his choice.

It is a game for him, but one I am ready to learn.

So I am in a barn, sheltered and hidden away, some fair distance from the manor but close enough that he may visit me when the need takes him.

It is often, but not as often as my own need.

'Often I mused upon you,' he says one night as we lie in the sweet-smelling hay in the loft, 'sealed away in your cell, where I could steal no glance at you to find what manner of woman you were.'

At first I turned my head away from the heat of his glances, which were in no wise stolen but rather bold and stealing, robbing me of all modesty. But now I wait for his gaze, and meet it, and tell him things he is glad to be told. My wretched coarse gown he has taken away, and in its place I have some fine linen and a warm blanket of rough cary cloth. When I wash the linen or myself I must do so in the stream which runs down past the house and then on through the gully by what was once my cell; and must do this only at night, when there will be no one to see. I am his secret diversion, imprisoned here as I was once imprisoned in that cell.

When I ask, he tells me that no other recluse has wished to enter the cell. It has been declared unclean. And there is no one now to intercede for the peasants and sinners.

I too am a sinner, I who renounced the evils of the flesh and now am prey to those evils and welcome them. I am in sin and afeared of what may befall me. But I am most cast down not when the man is using me but when he is not there across that tumbled hay, not here beside me, and I go hungry. All this, laughing, he knows.

But often he waxes serious and we talk as man and wife might talk, and I pretend it is so. We walk at night and he finds I can talk of many things beyond his own knowledge. I have had those many years for meditation and for listening to the prayers and problems of serf and freeman, and there is much I know. But too much I still do not know.

Once he speaks of love and then tries to laugh it away. But I am content that the jest should have been made.

Now the weeks pass and he comes no more. For the first time I see another man. I am fed by a serf who would like to make mock but dare not; and, I am bound, would relish the telling of jokes to his fellows, but knows he will have tongue and ears cropped if he so much as whispers of me.

And when at last my true master returns, he is graver than before but will speak nothing of his concerns.

Now I carry his child. This I have known for weeks but have waited until there shall be no mistake.

Now surely it is time that he declared me to the world? For he loves me, I am sure it is true: and if true only when he is with me, then that is truth enough, and all the greater reason for my asking that he shall be always with me.

When he hears and believes, he laughs. It is not the old laugh nor a gentle one. I would dare swear he is frightened, which I have never seen in him till now. And, being frightened, he grows angry and hateful.

I am a fool. How should I be other than a fool? I have spent much of my life away from the world in one secret place and now have let time run by in another such place, learning one thing in one and another thing in another, but still learning little of the ways of the world.

For of course as a Brobury he must marry the daughter of a neighbour so that as they unite then also their manorial lands may be united. Wherefore his dalliance with me is ended. How should it be otherwise?

175

I am to be sent away with a gift to ease the parting. But I must go in secret and not return and not speak of this. He promises that we shall meet later but I think it is of no importance to him. Once I have gone he will find other sport. He is as impatient for me to be gone as he once was to possess me.

All this I must accept. But as the fever came upon me in my cell and in my lonely mind, to fill my imaginings with a fearful joy, so a fever comes on me again and I am in a rage against him and will not let him go and am of a mind to go out across his father's lands like a wandering mendicant, telling all I meet of my fate and of the firstborn child he shall have by me.

This is folly indeed. Now it is all turned against me and I see I am in danger from all of it: his fear, anger and hatefulness. From the passion that is now the passion of hatred.

I will not be led away by him or by his servants. It would be too easy, in those woods and copses and hidden vales on the Brobury estate, for me to be struck down and buried where none will ever seek for me. That is what I read in his eyes – eyes which I have known lustful, eager, loving . . . and now murderous.

When he has left me this night it is easy for me to leave on my own way. I have no possessions, nothing to carry but his child within me. Beyond the hills where no word of me has been noised there may be those who will take pity.

Yet even as I silently depart and walk in darkness up the slopes I know I shall not need to go far. In the woods below the hilltop there waits for me what has waited a long time.

I remember. I remember the secret woods and the secret people who cared for me and taught me their ways. I remember those who crept up from the valleys to dance silently round the sacred places and offer their sacrifices, and those who took back from the rites the consecrated branches and their undying thoughts.

It was as if the knowledge had been in my mind all my life, waiting to be awakened. Here was the old true religion of my ancestors, anathematized by Roman, Saxon and Norman but enduring and unconquerable.

The old ones have never really deserted us.

I have been wronged, and the father of my child is not one of us, but still in the all-mother's mercy the child shall be cleansed and dedicated.

It is my own wish that the dedication to Ceridwen shall be made where I was granted the first intimations of the truth. I shall be sustained now by the truth, and bear my child before the stone of the sacred well. There I was imprisoned and then found freedom; and now of my own free will I return to cleanse it by the birth of my child and the rebirth of the old truth.

The stone is there, within the cell. I am in pain, I cannot set one foot before another save with pain, but I shall be given the strength to reach the place.

It is so close now, and the stone mother waits there to bless the mother of flesh.

But it is not to be. As I am stricken to the ground by the joyous agony of the child's coming, the night is full of them – of Brobury kinsmen and their hirelings, tearing the baby from me before I can kneel to Ceridwen, before the ash and oak leaves can be most propitiously laid out. I hear one cry – the cry of birth – and then my own cry, and then there is a bloody darkness and I am thrown this way and then that way, and there are voices thundering denunciations at me. My arms reach out but are empty. I am dying. And I know that my child is dying, and feel within myself the moment of his death.

He is gone.

And when I can hear and see, there before me is the priest in the full panoply of his self-righteousness, telling me that God is just and merciful and has taken unto himself the fruit of my sin. I must pray. There is nothing left for me now but to pray for the soul of my lost child and, in the hope of mercy, for my own soul.

Oh, I will pray. But not to their usurping idols. The truth makes me strong even in this moment of despair and humiliation.

They accuse me of abominable practices and heathen sacrifice, and it is proclaimed that for my own good and that of the faithful I am to be walled up alive and spend what little time is left to me in repentance. So I am thrust back into my cell and the wall is built up solid, even to the window, and I am in darkness and there will be no light and no food and my time will not be long. Day and night

177

without cease there come brethren to pray and chant so that none may hear the prayers I cry out at them, until I am too weak to cry any more, and when they are quite sure I am close to death they offer up a last prayer and depart.

So I die. Yet will not die. I do not rest and will have no rest until the child stolen from its rightful altar is avenged. They tried to sing down the curse I laid upon the Broburys, but could not undo it. There shall be no peace for the Broburys, and their womenfolk shall turn upon them as the traitors they are, until a firstborn is offered back to the sacred stone.

It is to be fulfilled. I walk through the pathways they have made, and with each step I am nearer to the stone and nearer to my time. The boy is eager to be free from me. A child was offered to Ceridwen as fruitful mother of earth, but Ceridwen was robbed. Now the balance must be set right. This Brobury child is offered to Ceridwen the destroyer and devourer.

She waits, stone mother with stone knife, upon the stone which was once my floor.

So few steps to take now.

Bronwen knew Judith and knew Matilda, allowed herself to be Judith and Matilda in this timeless swirl of past and present, without obtruding one vestige of her own self. She saw through their eyes and felt through their skin. And she felt every increasing, quickening pang of the child within the body that had become as much her own as Judith's – or the guiding, dominant Matilda's. Of the three of them, Judith was the weakest. Judith had surrendered mind and body to the spirit which had been waiting in this grove for so many centuries – had given flesh and power to the wraith whose vengeance was so close now to fulfilment.

Through Judith's ears Bronwen heard the rustling and faint, hungry whistling between the hedges. Judith looked straight ahead, but was calmly aware of the shadowy tremor of leaves and branches as heavy bodies blundered against them from the other side. They were all of them, women and beasts, making their slow predestined way to the stony heart of the maze.

Matilda knew what waited there and saw it adoringly in her mind;

178

so that Judith, too, saw it ahead and went on towards it; and Bronwen was with her.

They saw Lady Brobury utterly still, with a face of stone, cross-legged upon the cell floor with a broad stone-bladed knife across her knees. Her eyes were slits, her mouth a slit almost ready to open.

Bronwen flinched. But it was her own mind that rebelled, without striking the faintest echo from the others. She could lie dormant no longer. She had come this far without disclosing herself. But now Judith must be torn free from her trance. Whatever the dangers of such a mental shock, they were less than the dangers waiting at the end of this last avenue.

Bronwen reached out and declared her presence, demanding that Judith should hear her and stop, look round, discover herself again.

Three women in one, they went unfalteringly on.

Judith, listen to me. She must be shaken into consciousness, must hear and understand the meaning of those hungry noises behind the hedges: turn and walk back to the entrance.

Judith passed a side alley of the maze without a glance.

Bronwen struck savagely out into that captured mind. *Turn back. I am holding your hand, you must feel that I am holding your hand and turning you round. Like this. We will walk back together. Now!*

Judith, neither listening nor rejecting, walked on.

Bronwen struggled to convey the sensation of another, outer world. She would make herself feel the grass beneath her and hear the sound of the stream by which in reality she knew herself to be sitting – and would make Judith feel and hear it too.

She bent her will to the summoning up of that awareness.

And felt only what was in Judith's mind, and felt her birth pangs.

Bronwen tried to cry out. But Judith was mute.

They were held, both of them. Bronwen, too, was trapped in the web of the past. She could not draw Judith out of it; and could not even free herself. They walked on, driven by Matilda and all she had known and all she had left resonating on the air of this haunted place.

There was no escaping now. She must endure it all, to the end.

3

The ostler mistrustfully picked at the mole on his chin. He had been on the verge of lowering the bar across his stable-yard doors, and now resented the delay.

'Wouldn't fancy one o' my nags being ridden off over the top there, not by a stranger, not when it's dark as this.'

Caspian said: 'It's a matter of life and death. I have to get there as soon as possible.'

'And wouldn't do it no good being hard pressed, neither. You'd do better going round the road – and even then, this time o' night it's no easy ride for a stranger.'

'I'll guarantee whatever extra fee you want. But I can't stand about here, I've *got* to get there.'

Still the man dawdled. Caspian longed to take him by the throat and shake him as one would shake a rat. But that would hardly endear him to the fellow.

'Well, if I could be sure you'd be sticking to the proper road, like ...'

The train from which Caspian had alighted let out a croaky whistle and pulled away from the station. As the level-crossing gates swung back, a woman in a creaking little donkey-cart drove out from the lane beyond the station and clattered in beside the ostlery. Hunched over the reins, it appeared that she was urging herself and the animal on; but when she stopped and spoke she still did not straighten up, and it was evident that she was permanently stooped forward.

'Evenin', Ben. You seen my boy about?'

The ostler shrugged a shoulder at her and shook his head in much the same welcome he had offered Caspian. Remembering the man's joviality a few days previously, Caspian could only assume that there were moods in which he enjoyed pleasing customers, and others when the world disappointed him and he wanted everyone to suffer with him.

'Not today,' he grunted. 'Nor yesterday, now I think on. Nor God knows when.'

'He told me they'd be expecting me over there at Ladygrove about now. Reckoned her time would come today, but nobody ain't sent for me.'

'Then it's not come. Or they made other arrangements.'

'And who'd do better than me? I ask you – who'd do them better?'

The ostler parried. 'Didn't I hear the lady was going away?'

'According to my boy, she was sure to come back when her time'd come.'

The ostler said grumpily: 'Looks like everyone's set on getting to Ladygrove. This gentleman, too, he's in a mighty hurry.'

The old woman's eyes peered out keenly and acquisitively from under the scarf knotted about her head. 'Would that be so, then? You've heard something, is it?'

'I know young Lady Brobury needs help.'

'Just what I was saying.' She was triumphant. 'Knew it in my bones. So I'm not waiting to be sent for, I'll be off and see how she's faring.'

The ostler allowed himself to cheer up. 'You could take this gentleman with you. I'll tell you, sir, you'll be safe enough with Mrs Morris. Knows every road hereabouts, and she'll not waste a minute getting you there.'

'Ain't never been late yet,' the woman said. 'Least of all on this kind of work.'

She patted the seat beside her, grinning an invitation. Caspian sprang up.

'Shall I take the reins?' he asked, making a polite offer out of his desire to get his hands on them and force the pace along the winding route to Mockblane and Ladygrove.

'I've handled it often enough, thanking you all the same.'

When they set off he had to admit it was true enough. Mrs Morris set a confident, spanking pace, knowing every twist and rise and fall of the road, slowing and then taking a tight corner, urging or holding back the donkey with perfect calculation. Still he raged with impatience and fear, longing to annihilate the distance between here and whatever might be happening to Judith Brobury.

And to Bronwen.

If she had disobeyed him, had emotionally thrown herself headlong into Judith's mind and problems . . .

'There's been a sight of coming and going at Ladygrove,' said Mrs Morris chattily. 'You had any part in it, then?'

'My wife and I were staying there until a few days ago.'

'Oh, that'd be you, would it? Yes, my boy told me there was folk there.'

'Your son's on the staff?'

'Not my son. My grandson he is, sir. My poor daughter Lily's boy. Evan, we called him. She didn't live long enough to give him a name of her own.'

'I'm sorry.' Then, shaken, Caspian said: 'Evan? Not Evan Morris?'

'You've met him, then?' The old woman glowed.

'If it's the swineherd who – '

'That's what he's doing for them now, yes. Indeed. Evan Morris it had to be, 'cos there weren't no father to give the lad his name – not one that was going to own up, that is, though he wasn't mean with the money to help me along with him. No, you couldn't say he was mean.'

They swerved round a corner, the oil lamps casting a flickering glow on the donkey's flanks and on the hedgerows which lurched closer and then fell away again. Only once did they encounter another traveller, a man shuffling along and somnolently blurting out the odd belch of a refrain as he swung his lantern to and fro. And once, just as they turned the end of the vale and crossed a bridge which would lead them on to Mockblane and another bridge, there was a distant red cough in the sky from an engine's fire-box.

Caspian said: 'It was you who brought Evan up – and put him into service with the Broburys?'

'They took him without me or Mr Morris having to ask. Only right, when you think of it. There at the start, you might say, so who'd got a better right to stay on there?' She was driving more recklessly, but Caspian was in no mood for her to slacken the pace. 'A night like this, it was.'

'When he was born?'

'I was a sight younger then, when I was called over to bring him into the world. Came on very sudden, he did. It was that as much as anything, him coming early, that killed her. My own daughter, and one of the few I ever lost.'

'You were sent for because – '

'Because everyone sends for me, why else? I've delivered nearly every babe you'll find round these parts. Hardly a one in Lenhale or Mockblane I haven't brought into the world. And my own daughter one of the few I couldn't see safely through.'

Mrs Morris began to snivel, and the cart swayed perilously close to the ditch on an unfenced corner. Caspian reached over and tugged skilfully on a rein. When they were safely back on course he drew a hip flask from his back pocket.

'A drop of this will warm you.'

The woman cast it a sly glance, then resumed her concentration on the road. 'Best not, with the work I may have to do.' Her gaze strayed again. 'Wouldn't want to get like old Dr Treharne, would I? Hope they've not called *him* in. Wasn't none too sober when he did that inquest on Sir Mortimer, was he?'

'Was he not?' said Caspian – too keenly, for she clicked her tongue at the donkey and pretended not to be interested in the flask in his hand. Then, succumbing, she said:

'Well, just a little warmer wouldn't do no harm, would it?'

He filled the cap and passed it to her.

'When I think of our Lily and him . . .' Mrs Morris drank half the brandy, tightened the rein, and then drained the cap. 'Our Evan. If everyone had his due . . . But then, I'll not be a tittle-tattle.'

Caspian took the cap from her, and she said, 'No, I oughtn't to take another drop from you, sir,' and he refilled it and she took it gratefully from his hand.

'If everyone has his due?' He altered her phrase slightly, temptingly.

'After all these years, I don't suppose it makes no odds. And he's dead and gone.'

'Sir Mortimer?' Caspian hazarded.

'I never said a word, now.'

'Your grandson's father,' he said.

The shoulder of the hill against the sky was familiar now. A few dim lights in the valley marked the windows of Mockblane. Mrs Morris flicked the reins, and her tongue chattered encouragement along the backs of her uneven teeth.

'Evan is Sir Mortimer's son, isn't he?' Caspian insisted.

She passed the empty cap back to him, and wiped the back of her hand appreciatively along her mouth. 'Well, after all these years . . .' She giggled, and at the same time made an effort to straighten her bent back in a thrust of family pride. 'Oh, yes, if everyone had his due!'

'When was he born?'

'Before *he* was. Maybe only a day or a day and a half, as I recall, and ahead of time he was – but before Sir David, as that one calls himself. And maybe my Lily was only a slavey, but she was good enough for Sir Mortimer when the fancy took him. And it took him often enough, the Lord knows, specially when that lady of his was carrying and hadn't got no time for him. So why shouldn't our lad have been Sir Evan? Or maybe they'd have called *him* Sir David.' She shook her bowed head, bemused. 'But it don't ever work out like that, does it?'

They were rattling through the village. Light glowed in the window of the inn, and a curtain flickered in a corner cottage as they turned down towards the bridge.

Caspian was tense, pleading, reaching out ahead for some intimation of Bronwen.

The donkey slowed on the hill, then was in through the gateway.

'Stop here!' said Caspian.

'I'll set us down at the door and – '

Not stopping to argue, Caspian vaulted out of his seat and came down heavily on the grass verge of the drive. He ran down the slope to the huddled shape which might have been a bush on the edge of the stream but which he knew to be Bronwen. Sliding down to the cold, wet grass beside her he touched her hand; and found it as cold as death.

As his hand moved over hers, so his mind settled beside hers and then gently embraced it.

And was jerked galvanically in a moment of stabbing torture before he could steady himself and hold firm.

In the middle of torment Bronwen knew he was with her at last, and sobbed her love. If on the journey here he had been pricked by anger at the thought of what risks she might madly have taken, and now saw how truly she had lost herself in a consuming hell, that was banished. They were together in the web and must be together to the end. They were in tune. He enfolded her, she enfolded him, they would need all their strength.

There had ceased to be any true consciousness of Judith or Matilda. There were no longer any individuals. All their minds seethed and began to dissolve in the same fearful cauldron.

Caspian clung to his wife. There was no firm ground, yet they must be firm. They must retain their identity or they would be engulfed.

As if the walls of the anchoress's cell had turned to glass, they saw within it Lady Brobury, possessed by what she had so long and so devoutly invited. The slits of her eyes were opening; the eyes were gleaming jewels. Her mouth drooped, slack yet avid. Saliva trickled from one corner down her jaw like the glistening path of a snail.

Moving closer at his mistress's command was Evan Morris, neither person nor spirit but a mindless gape of murderous greed, as predatory as the animals which followed him from the dark interstices of the maze.

Bronwen and Caspian spoke Judith's name silently, beseechingly, repeatedly.

They had almost reached the end of the avenue. The woman with the stone knife waited.

Through every muscle and the straining flesh they could feel Judith ready to sink to her knees as the child fought to get out; but could not hear her mind or get any grip on it.

And blustering in as if to thrust them deeper into the cauldron and drown them, the weight of Evan Morris splashed with all the bestial ferocity of the great boars crashing through the hedges.

Suddenly a mental shout was torn from Caspian.

Judith, your son is not the one. Stone mother, sow goddess, avenger and destroyer, she has no call on your son. Not while a firstborn still lives.

Rage bubbled about them. He felt that great claws were tearing confessions from the depths of his mind, and tearing the soul out of him at the same time. Lady Brobury's right arm was dragged up with infinite slowness as if flexing anguished life through unyielding stone. She raised the knife, but the blankness of her face was that of bewilderment.

There is a firstborn here, a firstborn Brobury of another generation, before this.

From pandemonium thundered a cosmic question. Lady Brobury staggered under the flail of the answer. And out of chaos the Caspians heard Judith at last, whimpering as she groped to the surface of her trance.

Turn aside . . . now!

With all their power Caspian and Bronwen conjured up a vision of a hedge blocking that final, fatal avenue. They saw it and made Judith see it. Insisted to her that there was no way ahead. She faltered. The maze was warped, knotted into a new complexity. Judith could not walk ahead, there was no path, she must turn.

She stumbled to the left. They made an opening for her in their minds, and the opening became real and she felt her way into it.

As far in as you can go. Lie down there, stay there, you are safe. Stay there and you will be safe.

A furious enemy tore at the picture they were creating and slashed it across, mangled it and threw the fragments on to the storm wind. But Judith was already collapsing at the end of the cul-de-sac. The child's head was emerging. She could not get up now, and it was too late to drag her to the stone floor where what had once been Lady Brobury crouched, rearing up, howling in the insane abandonment of evil.

Evan Morris was confronting the priestess, his arms outstretched, raging, demanding the fulfilment of her promises to him.

The stone blade was raised.

'You will serve.' Lady Brobury was drawn up to her full height. 'If you are the one, then let it be you. *You.*' The shout drove the knife down. Morris stood quite still, held by the stone stake lodged in his heart. In that last instant the eyes staring at him were Lady Brobury's, wide and pleading for meaning. 'So be it, then, so be it. Let it be done thus and let there be an end to it.'

Morris crumpled. Lady Brobury, still clutching the haft of the knife, was drawn down with him. Then her fingers slackened, so that he fell free and rolled off the edge of the smooth, shining stone.

There was a whistle of triumph. Two huge boars hurled themselves bodily through a hedge. A frenzy of tusks and foraging snouts followed, descending on the corpse, treading and trampling into a mass which was tugged and chewed out on to the ground.

Lady Brobury went down on her knees.

The heat of the stone floor was dying away, cooling.

When the nightmare too had lost its heat, Bronwen and Caspian freed themselves and rose to their feet on the bank of the stream. Across the bridge and into the grove and the maze they went to face the reality. They found Judith sobbing quietly but happily above her wailing, new-born son, and Bronwen shed her cloak to wrap it round the child and carry him out into the world.

And Caspian found Lady Brobury, still kneeling, with her eyes still wide and unknowing, and her mouth twisted in the last petrified spasm of death.

✤ 4 ✤

The stone slab was prised away by picks and crowbars to reveal a wide round hole and the shaft of a well. The estate workers who had freed it backed away, leaving it to Sir David Brobury and Dr Caspian to lean over the rim and peer down.

Although David had ordered the demolition of the entire cell, so that the centre of the maze was now only a heap of rubble and the site was open to the sky, still the daylight struck only a short way down the exposed shaft. A lantern was brought and lowered on a rope. It shone on the sides of the well and dropped a glimmer like a dull coin into the muddy water at the bottom.

'Obviously fed by a subterranean inlet from the stream,' commented Caspian. He glanced over his shoulder to make sure that the workmen were out of earshot. 'And if it's Celtic, it would have been revered as one of the gateways to the underworld, and suitably guarded.'

Halfway down, the lantern revealed an earth-spattered skull in a niche to one side. When the light was swung round it fell upon a companion across the shaft.

Later in the day, some clumsy fishing with a bucket brought up votive offerings of stone and iron arrowheads, and one small stone figurine from which they had to wipe away a long accumulation of mud.

The effigy was that of a woman with grotesquely inflated breasts and hips, and a small head with pitiless slits for eyes and mouth.

David Brobury shivered. 'I want that taken away from here,' he said. 'As far away as possible.'

'I'm sure the British Museum will be delighted to accept her,' said Caspian.

It was tacitly agreed that the figure should not be shown to Judith.

'And I shall have the maze torn up,' said David, 'root and branch.

Just suppose that Judith had been in there, in one of those moods of hers, when those swine stampeded . . . no, I'll have the maze and the herd exterminated.'

He said it again when they were sitting at Judith's bedside that evening, having admired the healthy-looking son and congratulated the pale but contented mother. Judith looked momentarily puzzled, trying to remember something that did not quite fit what David had been talking about; but then leaned back luxuriously among her pillows.

'Since you were unfortunate enough to witness some of what happened' – David looked across the bed at Caspian – 'could you possibly stay on for the inquest?'

'Of course. We'll . . . give as accurate an account as possible.'

'I still can't believe it. I can't see how . . . and how I could have slept all through it, and the rest of you come back and . . .'

'The coroner will almost certainly find,' said Caspian levelly, 'that the herd for some inexplicable reason ran wild. There's little enough left of Evan Morris to identify, and what there is tallies well enough with that assumption. And coming on the scene, your mother died of a heart attack.'

'Exactly. Because that's just what happened, isn't it?'

With hardly a hesitation Caspian said: 'It must have been.'

'Sit with Judith a while, will you? I'll go and settle one or two things.'

When he had left the room, Judith picked thoughtfully at the frilled edge of a pillow. At last she said: 'I'm so grateful to you both. I still don't understand, but I know – somehow I know – that if it hadn't been for you I wouldn't be here, I wouldn't be – '

'It's over,' said Bronwen. 'Don't try to remember.'

'But I do keep trying to remember. It's all so strange, I seem to see things, and if I close my eyes I start a sort of dream, and then it's all gone again.'

'Let it go.'

'Somebody . . . something . . . wanted my baby. And if it hadn't been for you – '

'It was a terrible dream,' said Caspian, 'and it's over. You have David, you have your son.'

189

'But poor mother – '

'Is at rest.'

It was a platitude, the old conventional catch-phrase. He could only hope it might be true. *Between the stirrup and the ground I mercy asked, I mercy found.* If it were not so, and there were no forgiveness...

Bronwen said: 'Think of the future, and of young ... but have you decided what you're going to call him?'

'Alexander,' said Judith.

Caspian tugged at his beard, embarrassed, and both women laughed.

'Because,' said Judith, 'although I don't know quite what you did, or why it had to be done, I know that my son has to be named Alexander.'

It was that night, after they had dined and raised their glasses to the future of this young Brobury and the other young Broburys there might later be, that Bronwen said gently to her husband:

'And how shall we name *our* child?'

'There'll be time enough to worry about that when we've decided to have one.'

'The decision was made,' she said, 'that night in Wales.'

He stared. 'But it's too early to tell.'

'Not for us. I know it's so.'

She drew his mind into hers. Their rhythms clashed, went into a drumming counterpoint as he resisted and refused momentarily to believe, and then fell into a peaceful unison.

'Yes,' he said aloud.

And silently he told her she was right, of course she was right and he knew and felt all she felt.

'But what may a son of ours inherit?' he asked.

'Or a daughter.'

'A child who could read its parents' minds ...'

'No,' he laughed, 'oh, no!'

She was caught up in his alarm, and in his doubts, and in a sudden fear that their own unique closeness would be despoiled and invaded. Then they were both swept up in a tide of love and laughter, knowing that from all that was good between them there could come nothing that was not even better.